JOHN & CAROLE
BARROWMAN

INQUISITOR

HEAD
ZEUS

First published in the UK in 2018 by Head of Zeus Ltd
This paperback edition published in the UK in 2019 by Head of Zeus Ltd

9 7 5 3 1 2 4 6 8

A catalogue record for this book is available from
the British Library.

ISBN (PB): 9781781856475
ISBN (E): 9781781856444

Typeset by Ed Pickford

Printed and bound by CPI Group (UK) Ltd,
Croydon, CR0 4YY

Head of Zeus Ltd
First Floor East
5–8 Hardwick Street
London EC1R 4RG
WWW.HEADOFZEUS.COM

INQUISITOR

JOHN BARROWMAN is an entertainer with a career that includes theatre, television, music and film. He is acclaimed for his portrayal of Captain Jack in *Torchwood* and *Doctor Who*, as well as playing Malcolm Merlyn in *Arrow*, *Legends of Tomorrow* and *The Flash*.

CAROLE BARROWMAN is an English professor and Director of Creative Studies in Writing at Alverno College in Milwaukee, Wisconsin. She also writes for the *Milwaukee Journal Sentinel*, the *Minneapolis Star Tribune*, and is the 'book guru' for The Morning Blend on WTMJ4 (an NBC affliate).

The siblings have collaborated on nine books and a number of comics. For more on their work visit www.barrowmanbooks.com

Also by
JOHN AND CAROLE BARROWMAN

Hollow Earth Trilogy

Hollow Earth

Bone Quill

The Book of Beasts

Orion Chronicles

Conjuror

Nephilim

To our readers,
imagine big things.

'The tree of knowledge is not the tree of life.'
Lord Byron

'Sing, Heavenly Muse...'
John Milton

You are invited

to a

gala concert performance of

'Black Orpheus'

St Peter's Square, Rome

Sunday

Invitation Only

1.

IN THE BEGINNING

When humans were divine and gods adored them, when time was not measured in hours, days, months or years, an angel fell from favour and was banished to Chaos. This fallen creature wandered in exile, watching the world through crevices in the darkness.

Soon the First Watcher was not alone. Others fell. They too were destined to watch the world in fleeting moments from their banishment.

Then the First Watcher discovered a rift that took him from darkness back to the light. Taking human form, he rose to power, seeking out three elements necessary to bring other Watchers into the light, to rule with him in a glorious Second Kingdom.

A golden lyre.

A sacred chord.

And a powerful Conjuror, whose magic would bring these elements together.

His enemies were prepared for him and his human legions, the Camarilla, and cast the First Watcher from his place of power. But they were unaware that he had left a seductive mark on the world, ready for the time when he might rise again.

That time had come.

ROME

623 BC

2.

FAMILY TIES

'Luca, it's time,' his mother said, waking him from sleep as the summer-solstice sky showered stars on the marshland outside the Servian Wall.

Dressed in unfamiliar robes, Luca found himself in a chariot, driving towards a moat of flames that circled the centre of the marsh. Another chariot raced beside him, its wheels a blur. He caught a glimpse of a girl, her wide eyes catching the firelight and her cloak spreading behind her like golden wings.

The chariots stopped together. Luca's mother lifted him down and set him on the marshy ground.

'Walk from here,' she instructed, on her knees next to him. 'Go to your father.'

She anointed Luca's forehead with oil, then nudged him towards the flames. He moved uncertainly, the smells of charred myrtle and ripe citrus making him lightheaded. He could hear the whole city's prayers echoing behind him like the weeping of a thousand crows. The girl in the golden cloak stood beside her own chariot, skin like copper and eyes fierce as a hawk.

'Come,' Sebina said.

Luca knew then that he would follow her anywhere. He took her outstretched hand and walked with her into the furnace. He felt nothing but a brush of warm air.

In the heart of the fire, a great silver tree stretched out of the marshy soil, its limbs like arms and its trunk pocked with hundreds of piercing yellow eyes. The eyes closed one by one, until only one pair remained. Unblinking. Focused on him and Sebina.

The eyes became part of a creature with wings of fire, its body covered in scales and swollen in the middle like the throat of a toad. Its head was human, mostly. The part that wasn't looked unfinished, like unformed clay. It spoke.

'Come to me, children. I will sanctify your powers. You will make me great again.'

Wordlessly Luca and Sebina walked into its embrace.

FRIDAY

ROME, PRESENT DAY

3.

SYMPATHY FOR THE DEVIL

The First Watcher had endured an eternity bound in a painting like a specimen in an apothecary jar. He stretched his gnarled fingers out of the canvas into the conditioned air of the sacred chamber. As each crooked finger broke through, his flesh snapped and sizzled like electricity before a wire burns out. He knew nothing about electricity, but he understood a great deal about burning: the reek of flesh when it seared to bone, the stench of everlasting terror.

The First Watcher had answered to a host of ancient sacred names: Afriti, Moloch, Scaramallion, Lucifer – and Inquisitor. His current favourite. It was a name that suggested sovereignty, arrogance, malevolence: all qualities the First Watcher admired and had rewarded in humans. He liked that the name suggested his dark personal relationship with the divine.

An alarm clanged double time.

The Inquisitor's fingers retracted in a whiff of foul air.

*

An acolyte of the Order of the Camarilla, dressed in a white hooded cassock with long bell sleeves, rushed into the secure vault, breathless and sweating. She stopped to let the heavy steel doors seal shut with a whoosh of air. A computer monitored the vault's humidity, temperature, and the painting's pulse. It was this third line of vitals, like sharp mountain peaks on the screen, which had caught the acolyte's attention. With a shaky swipe, she stopped the deafening alarm.

The First Watcher was awake.

The vault was a rectangular space the size of a shipping container. Surgically clean, it was dimly lit with only a ribbon of emergency lights on the floor. On the smaller southern wall, an arched grotto had been moulded into the steel walls, holding the painting in an ornate gold frame. The painting, a double portrait, showed a roll-top desk strewn with artefacts: a compass, a violin, a metronome and a stack of scrolls. The desk stood between the Inquisitor, cloaked in velvet and ermine and seated on a throne-like chair, and his disciple, Don Grigori. The surface where Don Grigori had once stood was flat and dull, the paint flaking away.

The edge of the canvas was glowing as if it had been outlined in neon yellow paint. With head bowed, voice trembling, the acolyte stepped close to the painting.

'Your Eminence?' she whispered. 'Your Eminence, can you hear me?'

The figure of the Cardinal was fluttering on the canvas.

'Your Eminence?'

A cloud of bluebottle flies coughed from the Inquisitor's painted smile. The question was faint, but distinct.

'Are you a believer?'

'I am,' replied the acolyte, kneeling before the painting.

The painting was pulsing now as if a human heart beat beneath the canvas. The Inquisitor's head stretched out into the vault, flesh dripping from his skull. His eyes dangled like onyx pendants from their sockets and loose skin hung from his thick jowls like lumps of suet. Thin strands of light kept his entirety harnessed to the canvas like a thousand fiery reins holding back a chariot. The grotesque face twitched.

'Are we ready?' his voice boomed, shedding flakes of thick paint on to the white concrete floor.

'We are close,' said the acolyte, 'but…'

'But what?' A second wave of fat flies spewed from the canvas.

'It is Luca. His commitment to our cause is weakening.' The acolyte paused and swallowed. 'His loyalty is unpredictable.'

The flies swarmed in spirals like a hundred tornadoes rising to the ceiling, choking the air vents.

'I will handle my son.' The Inquisitor's face swelled

10

before settling again, his tongue bleeding ochre onto the floor. 'What of the Conjuror? Is he finally ours?'

'Soon. The Conjuror and the lyre will be in our possession soon.'

The Inquisitor's gnarled hand shot out from the canvas, dragging the acolyte up to meet his slack, doughy face. 'No more failures. It is time to bring me back.'

She squirmed, panting, from the terrible grip. From inside one of her bell sleeves, she pulled out a sketch pad and began to draw, sketching and shading, her fingers a blur of light scoring across the page. She felt euphoric, like she was floating outside of herself, her cheeks flushed pink and her heart fluttering in her chest. She had been prepared for this moment since childhood. Like her father and grandfather before her, she was a blessed child of the Camarilla, her future inescapably linked to the Inquisitor's wellbeing, to his eventual metamorphosis. He was the source of her family's vast wealth and entrenched power. He was everything.

At first it looked as if the Inquisitor was being tugged unwillingly into reality, his wraith-like body still attached to the canvas. But suddenly the vault seemed to inhale, the walls sucking in on themselves; then exhaled again, its walls regaining their original shape, leaving the acolyte on the ground gasping for air. High on the ceiling, one by one, the fat flies ruptured, covering the chamber in foul buttery bile.

*

The Inquisitor had been bound for centuries. His flesh was weak, his muscles trembling. His time away had not strengthened his body the way he had hoped. He studied his hand with displeasure, its tissue-paper skin mottled with brown age spots, its veins like thin yarn running up his arm, its bones visible. His legs, too, were snaked with thin black veins that popped and bled through his skin when he tried to straighten his body and stand. His legs could not support his weight, feeble though he was, and he crumpled to the ground.

'Come, Eminence,' the acolyte whispered, lifting him. 'Let me help you.'

Swinging his arm over her shoulders for support, the Inquisitor shuffled towards the door of the vault. He tightened his grip, soaking up the acolyte's bewitching brew of terror and anticipation. She choked, turning as white as her robe.

'There now,' the Inquisitor murmured, absorbing all that she was and all she would become. 'Better. Much, much better.'

4.

ROMAN FEVER

On the other side of Rome, head down and a leather messenger bag bouncing against his hip, Callum Muir dodged clusters of tourists swarming the Piazza di Spagna. He couldn't risk his face being caught in the frame of one of the hundreds of photos being taken in front of the white steps Audrey Hepburn and Gregory Peck had made famous decades ago. He needed to stay off the radar for a few more hours.

Callum Archibald Mathieson Muir didn't want to be the thirty-fifth Earl of Dundonal. He wanted to challenge the destiny his birth dictated, to piss off his dad and the old-school expectations of what a Dundonal heir could be and should do. And so, a week before sitting his final exams at Edinburgh University, he had fled to Rome. In a city where – according to a Muriel Spark story he'd once read – artists were treated like gods, at last he could be the creative he'd always wanted to be. He didn't regret the decision, but survival without his substantial trust fund had required him to revive certain special… talents he'd developed during his years of classical education at posh Scottish boarding schools.

He'd also fallen in love.

In front of the crowded Barcaccia fountain, a young couple taking a selfie backed into Callum. He quickly ducked from their apologies, and cut to their left before bounding up the front steps of the three-storey town house next to the Spanish Steps that along with the Trinità dei Monti church anchored the historic neighbourhood.

He stood in front of the Keats-Shelley Museum's security pad, wiping his clammy hands on his trousers before punching the buttons. The panel pulsed yellow then flashed red.

Wrong code. Shit. The light flickered. Yellow. Wait. Wait. Thirty seconds before he could try again. He exhaled, calming his wired nerves. The meeting to seal the deal was only an hour away. He needed to get in and out of the museum fast.

He scanned the square. Expensive boutiques, designer shops, pricey flats and luxury hotels shared the public space with travellers living from their backpacks, musicians and artists busking their talents for a meal, budget newlyweds snogging on the steps, and crowds of tourists on discount tours, their colourful flags waving in the late afternoon breeze. A mobile phone store and a Starbucks nestled near the massive church that loomed over the square. Rome: rich and poor hand in hand, the ancient seducing the modern.

He noticed a busker bent over a guitar in the shade of a gelato cart on the far side of the fountain. She wasn't very good, picking Lou Monte's 'Roman Guitar' on her sticker-covered instrument, but she knew how to entertain, and a small crowd was gathering appreciatively, dropping coins inside the open case at her feet. The busker looked up, caught Callum's gaze, and smiled, sending a chill up his spine.

Was he being watched? Was someone on to his game? How was that possible?

The pad beeped. Callum punched the code again. Yellow. And. Red. Something was wrong. Concentrate. One last chance and he'd be locked out. Then, no matter the deal he'd negotiated, he'd have to cut his losses and run. He cracked his knuckles and rubbed the rough beard on his cheeks. He'd done this before. He knew the drill. Another thirty seconds, then get it right.

Relax, dude. Breathe.

The musician's song was plodding and slow, a sombre soundtrack to the day's bright August sunshine. Callum had never seen the busker in that spot before, and he'd been watching every day since setting up his cover as a volunteer at the museum. Every day he paid attention to the ebb and flow of the crowds, the peak tourist times for the museum, gaining the curator's trust, calculating when the time was right for their move.

His move.

He was alone now.

His breath caught in his throat as he swallowed his sorrow. His stomach rolled, reminding him he hadn't eaten all day. What else was new? His tall athletic frame had grown thinner since the accident, his jeans hanging loose on his hips. He popped a mint into his mouth, burped.

Should he run before things got any more complicated? Then what? Admit he'd failed? Go back to being 'Wee Cally' as if he were a character in a Roald Dahl story or the PG Wodehouse novels his gran adored? No. Not after everything that had happened in the last week. Callum cracked his knuckles, punched the code for the third and he hoped final time.

GLASGOW

5.

PICK UP THE PIECES

Later that same morning, Rémy Dupree Rush was staring out the tall windows of a Georgian mansion thinking about time travel. He later wondered if the idea had come to him because he was facing the past: Glasgow's Necropolis with its grey stone mausoleums, decorative Roman arches, Corinthian columns, and pencil monuments filling the view from the second-floor bedroom that had become his most recent home. Or maybe the idea had come to him because he'd spent the last two days pouring over his mother's journal again, convinced he was missing something that might change the awful trajectory of his life.

The day he'd sat numb and speechless at the Formica kitchen table in Chicago all those months ago was scarred in his memory. The day he had learned he was a Conjuror: a descendant of an African tribe with powers to alter reality with their songs and music. And not just any Conjuror. The only one left in the world.

He remembered the blood coating his mom's teeth after Tia Rosa's slap to her cheek to stop his mom from sharing her secrets. But his mom had carried on anyway, her eyes blazing with a teary determination. As Rémy stared out of the tall windows, her voice was as clear in his mind as if she were sitting next to him.

'I'm tired, Rémy. Tired of the noise in my head and the evil clutching my heart. It's time you get prepared for what's to come.'

The images etched on an ancient Roman frieze in the catacombs below the Tiber during his escape from the catacombs: that's what she had been referring to. The secret she'd kept from him. His destiny carved in stone – literally. The frieze had depicted the coronation of the King of the Underworld, and that King had looked a hell of a lot like him.

He'd spent the past few days scouring the pages of the journal, trying to find the rest of the words to the frieze inscription.

Ecce unus est...

These were the only legible words on the relief.

Behold! One is...

But 'One is' what? One is coming? One is going? One is caught in the Matrix? What?

Rémy sighed, rubbing the top of his shaved head. Of course, all this thinking about time travel might just have been inspired by bone-aching boredom. If he had to play one more frickin' game of poker or cribbage while under house arrest, he'd lose more than his shirt. Something drastic had to be done, if he was to put an end to this and make the Camarilla pay for murdering his family.

He went in search of Em.

6.

FRIEZE FRAME

Em Calder sat cross-legged in the sunroom at the back of the sandstone mansion with all the windows open out to the wildly overgrown garden, a late afternoon breeze rustling the pages of the sketchbook on her lap. Rémy watched her for a minute or two from the French doors off the dining room as she used the heel of her hand to add texture to a section of her drawing.

When he sat next to her on the wicker couch, he saw she was working on a sketch of him. Quickly, her cheeks pink, she closed the book. His gloom lifted a little. He liked Em. Maybe more than liked her.

'I think we should go back to Rome,' he said.

Em made a disbelieving noise, tucking the sketchbook under her leg. 'Why? We've direct orders from Vaughn and Jeannie to stay here until after their Council meeting. We can't risk another fight with that Nephilim.' She gently touched Rémy's head near a row of stitches from a nasty cut. 'You've not fully healed from the last one.'

Rémy took her hand, her warmth infusing him with confidence. 'I need to find out more about that altar frieze. I need to know what it means.'

Em didn't pull away. Instead, she opened her sketch-book with her free hand, flipping to a drawing she'd made. 'Take a look at this instead,' she said.

The frieze depicted two *stola*-draped goddesses standing on either side of the altar. One goddess held a set of pipes in her hands and the other clutched a lyre. Skulls frozen mid-scream, twisted tormented bodies, and flayed souls of the damned made up the high back of the throne in front of the altar while the seat itself appeared to be a cushion of wings, its legs constructed from broken bodies. Em had smudged that part of her sketch, but Rémy had it seared in his imagination. Because he was the one sitting on the throne of souls, and the Nephilim was crowning him with a laurel wreath.

'I don't want to study the frieze itself,' he said. 'I want to see its creation. I want to go *back*, Em.' He looked meaningfully at her. 'In time. To find out what it means.'

Em jumped up from the couch. 'That is *not* a good idea. My brother almost died the last time we time-travelled. You've seen Matt's eyes? They're like a kaleidoscope shifting at warp speed. What if next time his... I don't know... his entire head just *explodes*?'

'I don't think that's likely,' said Rémy as he followed her out into the garden. Despite its neglect, the tangled green space was flourishing with rose bushes in every shade of red and pink imaginable.

'Not taking that chance.' Em headed to the back of the garden and the shade of an oak tree where someone had hung a tyre swing.

'It's not your chance to take,' said Rémy, leaning against the tree as Em climbed on to the swing. 'Matt's as frustrated as I am with leaving so much unfinished, and you know Caravaggio will do anything Matt wants him to do.'

'Then why are you even talking to me?' Em swung higher, the tyre grazing Rémy's hip.

He grabbed the rope and pulled the tyre to a stop. 'Because I trust you more than your brother and I want... I think...'

'You think he won't do what you ask without me?'

Her proximity and the intense expression in her eyes spiked Rémy's pulse. Her unruly short hair caught the sun through the tree branches, its purple streaks looking like satin ribbons. What he really wanted to say to her was that he knew she would have his back, maybe more than her brother. But more than that, he wanted to say he was falling in love with her. And he was terrified that if he let her out of his sight before the lyre was found and the Inquisitor destroyed, he'd lose her like he'd lost his dad, his mom, and his aunt.

23

Instead he let the tyre go. 'You got me. I'm talking to you because Matt will do just about anything you ask him to do.'

Em smiled and jumped from the swing. 'You got that right.'

ROME

7.

MEMENTO MORI

On Callum's last try, the massive wooden door unlocked with a click. He stepped inside the small foyer, locked the door behind him and climbed the narrow marble stairs two at a time. At the top of the stairs, the landing was suffused with light from a high round window where centuries ago an attic might have been, its space long since demolished. To his left was a tiny gift shop and the museum office; to the right the entrance to the main room, a library panelled in dark mahogany with floor-to-ceiling shelves packed with leather-bound books and literary artefacts from the generation of English Romantic poets and writers who'd once lived in the house. Many of the most valuable artefacts were secured behind glass.

Flipping through a set of keys, Callum unlocked the double doors into the library. He inhaled the sharp smells of old books and lemon polish that permeated the fustiness of the windowless room. Once a sitting room where Percy Bysshe Shelley, his young wife and writer Mary Shelley, Lord Byron, John Keats, their friends and lovers worked and played (and in Keats' case died), its haunting aura quickened his pulse.

Many of Keats' manuscripts had been separated from their original folios when Keats died. His friends, fraught with grief, broke them up and distributed them among themselves as *memento mori*. It was to one of the cases near the separated manuscripts that Callum went right away. Easing a leather folder from his messenger bag, he untied it and spread a single illustrated sheet on the glass lid.

The ink woodcut was probably his best work since university, where he'd forged everything from letters home to parents to fake IDs, graduating to birth certificates and letters of recommendation from professors. Pietra had helped him see how he was wasting his talents. He took a deep breath.

The last time he'd seen Pietra had been in a seedy morgue, hours after a drunk scooter driver had hit her in heavy traffic on the Via della Conciliazione, killing her instantly and fleeing the scene. Finishing their treasure hunt had become his own *memento mori*.

Don't think of Pietra, he told himself.

He took one last look at the document's faded watermark: a strange family crest, a coat of arms with a flying stag at its centre that had given him the most difficulty. The copy didn't need to be perfect, it just needed to be good enough to delay detection of the theft. It would have to do. Time was up.

With the smallest key on the set, Callum unlocked the glass top on the wooden case. An alarm beeped softly under the lid, counting down the forty-five seconds for Callum to do what he had to do and get the case locked again. Reaching underneath the heavy lid, he carefully slid out the rare single sheet folio.

8.

RAISE A GLASS

Pietra had discovered the value of the illustration when they first settled in their flat in Rome. Unlike Callum, she had aced her exams at Edinburgh and been accepted to a post-doc lit and art programme at Sapienza, the University of Rome. She was researching the Rossetti family – Christina, the English poet, and her brother, Gabriel Dante, the Pre-Raphaelite artist – when she came across a reference to Lord Byron's 'Tree of Life'. Was it a lost poem perhaps? Priceless, if so. The answer to all their financial problems – but only if they could find it.

The day Pietra discovered a solid lead, they'd celebrated with a bottle of not-their-usual-cheap-piss Chianti.

'John Polidori was Byron's doctor and friend,' she told Callum breathlessly between kisses. 'In 1814 Byron needed to get out of England because of a series of sex scandals, and he allowed Polidori to tag along with him to Italy.'

'Like us,' said Callum, raising his glass.

'Like us,' Pietra agreed, 'only with servants, gold carriages, and much better vino.'

Callum shoved the pillow behind his head, staring up at the wooden beams on the sloped attic ceiling of their garret rooms. 'And who *wis he when he was at hame*?' Callum said, mimicking his gran's favourite phrase in his broadest Scottish accent.

Pietra rested her notepad on her chest and looked over at him. 'I do love when you talk dirty, *mio amore*.'

He set down his glass and crawled to her, nuzzling her neck, whispering, 'It's a *braw bricht moonlicht nicht*.'

She laughed, shoving him away. 'Let me finish.'

'OK. What does this Polidori guy have to do with Byron's lost poem?'

'That's the best part,' said Pietra. 'I don't think Byron's "Tree of Life" is a poem.'

Callum loved how passionate she'd become about this search, her intensity and focus overshadowing their continued dive into poverty and multiple bills that were past due. She refused to ask her well-connected Roman family for help, and he had no family he wanted to ask. His gran, maybe, but she'd tell his mum. No doubt about that.

Pietra gathered her long black hair into a loose ponytail. 'John Polidori killed himself shortly after he wrote an especially awful epic poem called "The Fall of the Angels."' She grabbed a book from the table. 'Look at this.'

'What am I looking at?'

'This illustration is the cover for the poem.'

'It looks like a tree from a Robert Crumb drawing.' Callum looked more closely. 'Are those people inside its trunk? Makes it look like the tree's shitting them out.'

'I think that's what it's meant to look like. Like they're being defecated from the world. And those images at the end of the branches look like ancient temples. But that's not the strangest thing about it.' Pietra tapped the caption.

Callum read it aloud. 'The Tree of Life marks the way to the Second Kingdom and its untold riches.'

'Look at the name at the bottom,' said Pietra. 'It's difficult to make out, but can you see?'

'Byron,' said Callum in surprise. 'I didn't know Byron was an artist.'

'Me either,' she said, shrugging. 'Not a serious one anyway. But everyone sketched and doodled back then, and that's why this drawing will be worth something to a collector.' Her eyes gleamed. 'And "untold riches" to us.'

'How?' Callum said uneasily, already guessing the answer.

'You're going to steal it and replace it with one of your forgeries. You'll have to get a voluntary job at the Keats Museum where the original is, of course. The Dundonal name can come in useful for once. With your talents, we could get away with it.'

Callum couldn't help himself. The thrill of working again, of flexing his unique artistic muscles was too much to resist. Plus, he'd flirted with their landlord as much as he could. Soon, they'd have to pay the rent.

He stood directly beneath the double skylights, noting the vines stretching from the bulbous trunk that looked like a prodigious bum and the pictorial glyphs etched on its main branches. 'OK, I'll bite,' he said, dropping the book and scooping her into his arms. 'Where is this Keats Museum?'

Pietra smiled. 'Right here,' she said as he carried her over to the mattress, kissing her neck. 'In Rome.'

*

Callum choked back the rest of the memory of that day. Slipping his forgery of Byron's illustration inside the case, he locked it, and silenced the alarm.

'No turning back now, *amore,*' he said into the silence.

GLASGOW

9.

AMERICAN PIE

In the front room of the Georgian mansion, Michelangelo Merisi da Caravaggio was about to skunk Matt Calder in a cribbage game that had the loser promising to cook dinner. Both men were drinking, Matt coffee and Caravaggio the previous night's sangria. Although the Orion safe-house was sparsely furnished, it had games, a stocked fridge, a big TV and encrypted WiFi.

Em loomed over her twin brother's shoulder. Born three minutes apart, the twins were as alike in their pale Celtic complexions and sharp features as they were unalike in their physical stature. Em was athletic but petite, while Matt was over six feet and built like a runner.

'Can't you let him win for once, Matt,' said Em checking the pegs on the cribbage board. 'Your spaghetti Bolognese isn't up to much, but Caravaggio can only cook one thing, and I'm not eating it.'

Matt's shades were up on his head, holding his long hair off his face. Tiny threads of gold flecked his kaleidoscopic irises. He regarded Caravaggio tipping on the back legs of the chair across from him.

'He's cheating, Em. You may get my spaghetti after all.'

Caravaggio tried to look hurt, but mostly just looked less mischievous, his dark eyes widening. 'That five of clubs caught in my sleeve. It was an honest mistake.'

Matt snorted, tossing his losing hand into the middle of the table. He stretched his muscles and walked to the windows at the front of the house. 'You win, Michele. I can't take any more card games. Were you yelling for me, Em?'

'I have a question for you to consider,' Em said. 'What if we went back to Rome with Rémy and you helped him to… "see"?' She put the word in air quotes.

'Don't do that,' said Matt, frowning.

'Hear her out,' protested Rémy.

'What if we were really quick?' continued Em. 'We don't need much time. We just need you to help Rémy figure out how his face got on to a stone frieze showing the coronation of the King of the Underworld.'

Caravaggio's feet dropped to the floor with a thud. 'I'm not going back into that Nephilim's lair,' he said. 'He wants to kill me, if you remember.'

Matt scratched his head with the leg of his shades, his eyes like stained glass, a jigsaw of colours. 'Rémy wants me to use my historical vision and replay a moment in ancient history when an altar frieze was created?' he

35

repeated. 'First, we don't know anything about where or when the frieze was created. And second, I need to be in the exact spot to replay anything.'

'What if we could find out where and when?' said Em, twirling a strand of her hair.

'How?'

'The library at the Abbey, back in Auchinmurn.'

Matt looked incredulous. 'But where would you even start?'

'With him,' said Em, pointing at Caravaggio.

The artist raised his eyebrows. 'Me?'

Em gave him a winning smile. 'Michele, before the Duke of Albion got you out of Italy on the day the world believes you died—'

'The day you stole a painting that the Camarilla had paid for,' Rémy cut in.

'I know what I did,' said Caravaggio, his expression darkening.

'You were… close to the Nephilim for a while,' said Em. 'You must remember something. A small detail about his past that may help us know why he's crowning Rémy in that relief.'

'Luca didn't talk in his sleep if that's what you're asking.' Caravaggio shifted over to the window sill next to Matt. 'The frieze represents the prophecy in the Book of Enoch: that a Conjuror will be crowned King of the Underworld and bring forth Chaos into this world.' He raised his eyebrows. 'Maybe Rémy's the real enemy after all.'

Rémy lunged, but the artist was quick and darted out of the way.

'If you're holding anything back, Michele, I'll kill you myself before the Nephilim gets his hands on you,' Rémy swore. 'You owe us.'

'He's right,' said Em, crossing her legs under her on the couch. 'We've let you roam free in our world for longer than we agreed. Don't push your luck.'

Caravaggio bowed deeply towards Em, but his body rippled with anger. 'I am most grateful for the extra time,' he said. 'But you know that I still need to clear my name and find the one who murdered my lover. That was my deal.'

'Come on,' Em scoffed. 'You've shown no interest in pursuing this supposed murderer since we met. You were full of shit then, and you're still full of shit now.'

*

The tension in the room screamed in Rémy's head. He stuck one of his earbuds in and tapped on the low static he kept on a playlist to cut through the strange eerie noises that haunted his head. 'With every step forward we take to try and stop the Camarilla, more people get hurt and more are put in danger,' he said tightly. 'I need to find out exactly what I can do to stop any more of that happening. So stop being such a prick.'

Em put her hand on Rémy's arm. He felt calmer.

'I've spent a lot of time in the last few days studying my mom's journal,' he said. 'And she really believed that if this Second Kingdom is allowed to rise from Chaos, then the world will become enslaved to the Watchers like they were demonic dictators, mindlessly following their rule and existing only to serve their needs.'

The others were silent.

'There is some comfort in not having to think for yourself,' said Caravaggio thoughtfully.

'Shut up,' said Em, scowling at him.

Matt rounded on her. 'Don't be a bitch.'

'Don't call me a bitch!'

Rémy shook off the clashing cymbals in his head. 'Listen to us!' he said in exasperation. 'Our nerves are frayed. *We* are not the enemy.'

The others quietened.

'Em and I can go to the Abbey and do some research,' Rémy went on. 'And Matt and Michele can go wherever and do whatever. But let's take a break from each other over the weekend and regroup on Monday.'

He could see the others were tempted.

'If Vaughn finds out we've left even for a day,' said Matt at last, his dark hair curling over the frayed neck of his vintage Bowie T-shirt that had once belonged to his dad, 'he'd never trust us again.'

'*If* he found out,' Caravaggio said. 'Given our recent pasts, there's reason to assume that he would.'

'Michele is right,' said Rémy.

'Since when do you side with him?' said Em to Rémy.

'Since he started agreeing with me.'

'We would need to visit an art gallery,' said Caravaggio who draped himself over an armchair. 'In case you haven't noticed, there's no art of any kind in this entire mansion that we could use to travel through.'

'It's risky,' agreed Rémy. 'We don't know for sure that Vaughn doesn't have someone watching us. But we have to get out of here, or we'll kill each other.'

'I'm hungry,' said Em, getting off the couch. 'Let's think more about this while we eat.'

'Do I have to cook dinner?' asked Matt.

'It would be my pleasure to cook,' said Caravaggio, unsheathing his knife from the band of his leather trousers.

'No way,' said Em, disgustedly. 'I'm not eating squirrel.'

'I'll do dinner,' Rémy said.

He slipped his harmonica from the pocket of his jeans, blowing a few notes to get their attention. Starting slowly with a riff from a Leon Bridges song, he then tapped his feet as the notes quickened in tempo. The music carpeted the bright airy room in a surreal multi-coloured mist. Suddenly the swirls of colour and the sounds took shape.

'Pepperoni on mine,' said Matt approvingly.

ROME

10.

WEEP NOT

With the original drawing safely in his messenger bag, Callum ducked into the museum's most visited room for the last time.

Directly above the first level of the Spanish Steps, Keats' bedroom contained the single bed in which the poet had died at the age of twenty-five from consumption: tuberculosis. Looking down from the wall was his death mask, created only hours after Keats' final breath by his closest friend, the artist Joseph Severn. Since Pietra's death, Callum had found himself drawn to the cloistered space.

The air in the room smelled musty and sour, but Callum felt a strange energy here, as if the vestiges of love and loss lingering in the room were calling out to him. Grief was a right hook to his head, hitting him hard and fast. He rarely saw it coming. Looking up through tears to see the painting of Joseph Severn bathing Keats with lilac water, dabbing the trickle of blood from the corner of the poet's mouth where it had settled after his final gut-wrenching cough, Callum felt the purest envy. He hadn't been so lucky. Pietra's casket had been closed, her heart sealed from him forever.

He wiped his sleeve across his face, admonishing himself for wasting precious time. Once the sale was final then he could grieve, preferably far away from here. He was meeting his buyer in an hour.

He had first met Fiera Orsini shortly before Pietra's accident, at her family's Trastevere restaurant, Osteria Armando. Ruthless in all her endeavours as her father and his father before him, people underestimated *La Madrina di Trastevere,* the Godmother of Trastevere, at their own cost. Signora Orsini knew Pietra's family and had seen samples of Callum's work, but had still demanded assurance of his veracity.

The day of their meeting, Callum had been seated at the only unshaded table on the apron patio. Pietra had warned him of *La Madrina*'s temperament. 'Do exactly what she asks,' she'd instructed him. 'Don't mess her around.'

Sucking up was usually not in Callum's repertoire, but he'd sat baking in the sun for two hours, sweat pouring down his back, his pale Celtic complexion getting redder and redder, until he'd spotted an elegant looking silver-haired woman standing at the wide sliding doors into the restaurant.

'For you,' said the waiter, handing Callum a linen napkin with a stack of euros wrapped inside. But when he had looked back at the doors, *La Madrina* was gone.

Callum turned when he heard footsteps on the museum's stairs. He could have sworn he'd locked the front door. He instinctively hid his satchel with its precious contents under the gift-shop counter. When he looked up, an older woman with mirrored sunglasses holding her hair off her face dressed in a white maxi dress was standing in front of him. At first glance, he thought her from the south of Italy, but when he heard her accent he wasn't sure.

'One please,' she said, digging in a Louis Vuitton bag for her wallet.

'I'm afraid we're closed today,' said Callum, combing his fingers through his hair, brushing away his despair.

She looked surprised. 'But the door was open. I'm leaving Rome tomorrow morning and I really wanted a quick look round. I promise I'll be fast.'

Callum glanced at his watch, suddenly feeling quite charitable. Now that he had the original illustration in his hands, he did have a little time before he had to leave to meet Signora Orsini.

'OK,' he found himself saying. 'But be quick.'

11.

TOUCH HAS A MEMORY

The woman paid her admission and bought a published guide to the museum. A twinge of anxiety jabbed Callum's gut as he escorted her into the wood-panelled main room. What was he doing? Why had he let this woman in?

'I studied the Romantics at university,' he said.

'What a coincidence,' said the woman, smiling pleasantly. 'As did I.'

Callum didn't believe in coincidences. Especially not today. Too much was at stake. He needed her out of the way, and he needed to get the hell out of there. She could see herself out. He was about to encourage her to browse on her own when he heard himself say: 'Let me get you started on the tour.'

The words kept coming, almost of their own accord. He told her of the museum's history, how Keats and his friends had rented it for the poet in the hope that Rome's air would keep the tuberculosis at bay. It hadn't, but the flat still became a salon renowned for the European literati of the time. Why couldn't he ask her to leave?

His phone beeped. The woman waved him off.

'Take it,' she said. 'I'll be fine.'

Callum returned to the gift shop and clicked on Signora Orsini's text message.

Usual place @ Noon.

His thoughts were clearer now that he was away from the woman. Grabbing the hidden satchel, he crept down the stairs to the front door – only to discover he had locked it after all. He reached for the brass handle, and yanked his hand back with a yelp. The knob was red hot.

He looked at his palm, biting back a howl. A raw imprint was seared into his skin, wet blisters already forming. He pulled the tail of his shirt out and covered his other hand. But before he could reach for the handle a second time, the entire lock-piece began melting, dripping like molten wax down the door and on to the tiled entranceway, a slight yellowish glow to the metal. What the hell was happening?

With his hand throbbing, Callum bounded back up the stairs and into the gift shop. He shoved his satchel back under the counter and grabbed a souvenir T-shirt, quickly wrapping his hand with it. He wasn't sure covering a burn was the best idea, but at least it dulled the throbbing and hid the watery blisters.

Loosening his tie and the top button of his white shirt, he took a deep breath to calm himself. Then he flew into the library to confront the woman. Who else could have destroyed the lock and trapped them both inside? He was going to be late for his sale.

She wasn't in the library any more. She was in the room with Keats' folios.

'Might I see one of these?' She tapped the glass case whose contents he'd robbed earlier. 'It would be so inspiring to get a closer look.'

Callum couldn't get any words to come out of his mouth.

'Are you hurt?' she asked.

'What?'

'Your hand?'

Callum stared, stupefied, at his hand. Why was it wrapped in a T-shirt? Carefully, he unwrapped it and stared at his palm. He wasn't sure what he expected to see, but it looked normal. The thin scar on the pad beneath his fingers where he'd sliced it when... when... the memory flitted away. He couldn't remember how he'd got the scar. He opened and closed both his hands. For a second, he wondered if he was having a stroke.

'The folios?' prompted the woman.

Callum's thoughts were foggy, and a dull ache was growing behind his eyes like the residual of a rough night, the pressure of a hangover. He couldn't seem to cut through the fuddle. Had he and Pietra finished the wine her father sent for her birthday? He didn't think he'd been partying. Pietra. Pietra. No. She was dead.

The woman touched Callum's arm. 'How about it?'

'I'm… I'm…' Callum stuttered. 'I can't unlock that.'

'Who's to know?' she said, squeezing his wrist.

She was right of course. No one would know. He'd gained the trust of the museum's curator weeks ago. A flush of heat drifted up Callum's spine and into his chest. He was sweating. He took a bunch of keys from his pocket. The dull ache thumping behind his eyes was a full-scale drum solo. He swayed where he stood.

*

'Get away from there this bloody minute!'

Callum looked down at his feet. Instead of his scuffed Italian loafers, he was in gym shoes, white shirt, striped school tie and grey shorts. More importantly, he was standing on one of the most treacherous ramparts of Edinburgh Castle.

'Callum!' yelled his dad. 'Don't move!'

Callum wobbled on the edge of the parapet. His foot slipped. His hands grabbed air. His dad lunged and grabbed his sweater, dragging him back over the wall, tearing his hand on the jagged stone.

*

The museum swam back into focus. Callum rubbed his thumb across the puckered scar on the pad of his right hand absently. He remembered now. He'd needed six stitches, and was taken back to school a week before spring term began, where he had sat alone at night sobbing, feeling sorry for himself and letting his anger at his dad fester.

He looked at his watch. Dammit. Forty minutes until his meeting with Signora Orsini and he was still in the museum. He stood up too fast, and floaters filled his vision.

In the small loo behind the gift shop, he splashed water on his face. His eyes were bloodshot and his nose was bleeding a little. He was drying his hands and face when he remembered the satchel.

12.

SUMMER DAZE

While Callum was forgetting, Lucius Ferrante was remembering.

He pushed open the shutters on the second floor of his townhouse on the northwest corner of Trastevere, welcoming a breeze inside for the first time in five hundred years. Spider webs fluttered like fishing nets from the ceiling and a threadbare tapestry rustled against a crumbling wall. Leaking water had stained the high ceilings and there were holes as big as fists in the skirting boards.

Despite the years of neglect and the ravages of time, the room was as Luca had left it. Ragged quilts on the regal bed were thick with grime, preserving the alabaster skeletons of the last man and woman he'd seduced, their bones tangled together in the filth as if waiting his return from the cellar with another flagon of wine.

It was the hottest month of summer, but a recent shower had soaked the uneven flagstones of the square.

Luca owned property all over the world, but this part of the neighbourhood was sacred to him. It was where he had experienced the greatest joys of his life and his deepest sorrows. Tilting his head towards the sky, Luca let the sun light up his face.

Home.

On the balcony that ran along the back of the house, he breathed in the scents of the piazza below: the rain-damp cobbles, the rich aroma of coffee from a nearby café, the succulent fruits and the perfumes of roses in plastic buckets, all neatly stacked under the arched portico of the Basilica di Santa Maria. The city's oldest Catholic church was built like so much of Rome on the foundations of its ancient glorious empire. An empire that Luca had pledged to see rise again.

His shoulder blades twitched at the rich scent of oranges. Suddenly alert, he scanned the square for the source. Not the vendors below. This scent was distinctive, ripe and full-bodied: an ancient odour. Above him he heard the *dubdubdubdub* of a helicopter hanging low in the sky, and admired the ingenuity that kept such a fat bug of a machine in the air. The helicopter banked towards the heliport inside Vatican City where it landed.

The smell intensified. And Luca knew the Inquisitor was in the world.

Time was running out for humanity.

In the piazza below, he watched a woman wiping bird shit from the steps of the fountain with napkins from the café before sitting to sip her coffee. Her daughter, a young girl of about five years old, was hopscotching on the cobblestones. Every two skips she'd stop and take a bite from a pastry in her hand.

'Careful, Ilarya,' said the girl's mother in Italian. 'It's slippery from the rain.'

The girl was jumping faster and higher, ignoring her mother's warnings. Luca closed his eyes and unfurled his wings.

Suddenly, the child screamed.

Her mother dropped her coffee and ran to her daughter on the ground. She scooped the child into her arms, scolding her and kissing her. 'I told you the stones were slippery, *cara*!'

'No, Mamma,' Ilarya said, rubbing a rosy mark on her leg. 'He knocked me down.'

The mother scanned the square, squeezing her daughter tighter. 'Who knocked you down?'

Ilarya pointed to Luca's balcony. The space was empty, tattered curtains billowing in the summer breeze. Puzzled, the mother looked more closely at the mark on her daughter's leg. It was a burn not a scrape, raw blisters erupting on the skin. What kind of person burned a child?

'Can you see the man anywhere?' she asked sharply.

'Silly. It wasn't a man,' said Ilarya, itching her skin. 'It was an angel.'

*

Having brushed the girl's leg with the silver tips of his black wings, Luca landed in a blur of light in a nearby square. Only certain people could see him in his divine form. Animare with their talent for bringing art to life, Guardians and their power in taming and shaping emotions, Conjurors wielding music like a weapon; and certain gifted children. Not because of their innocence or their susceptibility, but because the demands of the world had not yet cloaked their imaginations. Children didn't have supernatural powers, but they were free thinkers. Luca liked that. He hoped the girl and her mother would bicker all the way to school. Creating chaos in individuals' lives amused him. Opening Chaos itself was another matter.

Trastevere was a labyrinth of winding alleys and narrow corridors, punctuated with cobbled piazzas and garden patios. The morning sun was already baking the neighbourhood, brightening the colours and clouding the shabbiness of the shuttered apartments and the pastel-painted shops and cafés. Luca rolled his stiff shoulders. It always took a few minutes to adjust his posture from divine to human. His angelic form was closer to his human body than his true bestial essence. That he saved for special occasions. His shirt itched against his skin and his legs tingled, but these were feelings he knew would dissipate quickly.

When he was fully human, his musculature was tall and sculpted, his reddish-blond hair framing emerald eyes and high distinctive cheekbones. His skin was light brown and, since he had no body hair, looked translucent in direct sunlight. He threaded his way through packs of tourists strolling along the Via Del Moro. One or two caught his eye and he smiled, knowing he'd made their hearts skip, their breath catch.

A blonde woman in a short summer dress sloshed a mop on the stones in front of the newsagents across the narrow street, her forearms furrowed with ropey muscles, her calf muscles tense. Luca stopped at the end of the queue outside his favourite café. Drinking the strange dark brew was another of his trivial human pleasures. Cutting to the front of the line would be easy: a shoulder tap here, a wicked look there. But Luca's patience was unlimited. Time didn't concern him in the ways it rattled and jabbed at humans. He inhaled the heady mix of impatience, repressed anger, and polite submission that enveloped the queue, and revelled in it all.

The sun glinted off his silver-tipped cowboy boots, and the flash of brilliance for an instant fractured his indulgence. His mind went to Sebina, as it often did. He let his memories roll out, stoking his wrath against those who had taken her from him centuries ago.

ROME

1610

13.

METAMORPHOSIS

Luca crouched like a gargoyle on the ramparts of his castle's keep. Perched on a protruding water spout, his wings were folded against his broad back, his head down, his hands clenched in fists under his chin. From here, the Nephilim had a clear view over the walled Piazza di Santa Maria where Sebina was to be executed within the hour.

The alleys and streets surrounding the castle walls were unusually quiet. No men on horseback, no peasants hauling their wares, no vendors wheeling their carts over the stony ground. No patrons in gilded carriages, no prostitutes calling out to them.

The walled piazza and its surrounding townhouses belonged to the Trastamaras, one side of Luca's human family. As far as the world was concerned, Trastamara patronage ensured that the Basilica di San Pietro honoured the founder of the church of Rome. Luca knew better. The Camarilla knew better. The Christian edifice was a farce, a front. Built simply to conceal the sacred catacombs that protected the way to the Temple of Orpheus, and what lay beneath.

The crowd gathered in the piazza hummed with excitement. Luca squeezed his fists, searing his palms, the stench of his own charred flesh more tolerable than the amalgam of excitement, horror and lust rising from the crowd. Hundreds of torches blazed from iron sconces. The crowd was growing restless. They'd been promised a spectacle. Luca tightened his wings round his body. He would make sure they weren't denied.

He absorbed the darkness, letting it drape him like a shroud. Then he spread his wings and rose from the battlements, swooping over the chimneys and the uneven rooftops, landing with a fizz of pale light behind the statues of the nine muses on the Basilica.

There was a trumpet blast. Thanks to the artist Caravaggio and his cowardly disappearance, Luca was no longer the Imperial Commander of the Camarilla. His replacement marched out of the open doors of the Basilica and paused on the wide steps under the columned portico. The crowd cheered and Corso Donati lifted a hand in acknowledgement. Two legions dressed in red and gold tunics stood inside the walls, their heads shaved to the scalp to display the mark of the Camarilla.

The warm evening breeze brought a stringent whiff of body odour, overlaid with lavender – and the sharp scent of citrus. Luca's wings stiffened.

His father was here.

Donati signalled to a musician to blow the horn. The crowd sorted themselves quickly, marching in pairs into the Basilica. Luca dropped down on to the portico as the horn player, the last person to go inside, was pulling the heavy wooden doors closed behind him. He slipped past like a chill wind, into the church, where he flew unseen up to the highest gable above the altar. There, he folded his wings over his body and waited.

The sanctuary was ripe with orange blossoms that carpeted the altar. Below Luca's perch, the worshippers sat according to their social class and importance to the Camarilla's cause and the Inquisitor's plans. Seated first were the aristocracy: men and women wrapped in maroon silk cloaks whose descendants were the original patrician families of the city and whose ancestors had pledged their allegiance to the Camarilla. Behind them were the merchants and their families, and behind *them*, in black leather tunics and long capes, their identities hidden behind gold masks, stood the elite order of the First Legion: ten men and women, five Animare and their Guardian companions, whose duty was to protect the First Watcher. Luca's skin felt hot and his intentions began to waver. The presence of the First Legion meant his father was somewhere close.

The worshippers dropped to their knees as the bronze bull was wheeled down the wide nave. A brass bed layered with red-hot coals hissed and spat inside the bull, its eyes and nostrils spewing smoke.

The Inquisitor appeared behind the bull. His scarlet cape lay draped over a white lace and red silk cassock, his red pointed biretta covering his thick white hair, his hands clasped in front of him, and his enchanted pitch pipe hanging from a gold chain around his neck.

Luca's skin tightened. He pressed his wings against the fresco that covered the walls and ceiling, and watched Corso Donati lead Sebina in chains on to the altar. When he saw what the Inquisitor had done to her, his body buckled and his flesh softened. His humanity overwhelmed him.

Luca began to transform.

14.

BURNING GOLD

Sebina was dragged to the altar in chains, a hammered gold scold's bridle locked on her head to mute her screams and limit her powers, its weight pressing her head against her chest.

The scent of orange blossoms was making Luca ill. Sebina's will pressured him to stay out of sight, and he remained cowering on the massive beams in his naked human form. To his shame, overwhelmed with love for Sebina, he was paralyzed and powerless to act.

The Inquisitor sat on the throne in front of the altar.

'My son,' he called, pleasantly. The sound echoed around the Basilica. 'My dear Lucius, I know you are here somewhere. Heed this moment. When mistakes are made, retribution must follow. Nothing can come between me and my future, not even Sebina, my daughter. She has failed me. But you have a second chance. Nurture your anger, let it fester, and use it against the men and women who will thwart our divine plans.'

The coals beneath the sarcophagus blazed red-hot. Swarms of beetles scrambled up through the spaces between the planks of wood, pattering across the pews. The worshippers dropped to their knees.

Luca's mind filled with darkness as he thought of the artist. He should never have let Caravaggio escape.

Sebina's neck was bent awkwardly from the weight of the bridle, her flimsy blue gown trailing off her body like her soul in relief. Donati pushed her forward. Shrugging him off, Sebina dropped her gown on the altar, and climbed into the sarcophagus by herself.

Luca groaned in despair.

With the ability to skin walk – to alter her exterior like a creature of the desert or a deadly flower in the jungle – Sebina had always been impetuous and impossible to ignore. It was why Luca loved her. Dark-haired, brown-skinned like her mother, an Egyptian queen, she had a softness to her features that belied the toughness of her character. The memory of Sebina's fingers brushed his neck, her lips on his cheeks absorbing his tears, then her hand on his chest, and her whispers pledging undying love.

Donati slowly lowered the heavy brass lid of her scorching tomb. The flames beneath the sarcophagus hissed like a thousand snakes. The Inquisitor smiled up at the rafters, and bowed his head.

ROME

PRESENT DAY

15.

A POCKET FULL OF PEBBLES

A young priest sat at one of the café tables, head bowed, hands flat on the pages of the *International Herald Tribune*. An empty expresso cup and his mobile phone held down the corners of its pages. A slight breeze caught on the awning above his head, sprinkling a touch of the recent rain on to his newspaper, but he kept reading. From his position in the queue, Luca smiled to himself. Nothing in this world was that interesting.

The woman in front of him was wearing a scarf wrapped in swooping waves around her pale thin neck. In his head, Luca reached for the two ends and tugged until the woman's eyes popped. Amused at the thought, he tapped her on the shoulder.

'May I skip ahead?' he asked in Italian.

'Of course,' she replied, softening like wax.

An attractive male in a skin-tight T-shirt and skinny black pants was now directly ahead of Luca, swiping through his phone for the next perfect song. The man's chest was sculpted and his nipples poked at the flimsy material of his tee. Luca dreamily plunged his fist into the music lover's chest, tearing out his heart and dropping it at his feet. He blew cool breath on the man's neck.

The man turned in annoyance, saw Luca's smile and flushed.

'May I?' Luca said gently.

He slaughtered the rest of the line in increasingly inventive ways until he reached the barista, a youth with a sculpted beard and ears studded with silver. Luca's spirits were considerably more buoyant now.

'Sorry for the wait,' said the barista, whose name-tag said 'Thatcher' in bold script. 'Making a good cup of coffee takes time.' He swirled a fleur-de-lis into the snowy foam on the cup in front of him before adding with a laugh, 'Rome wasn't built in a day, you know.'

Thatcher's Italian was awkward and choppy, and his phrasing was punctuated with pauses at all the wrong places. Luca thought it was charming, and did nothing to correct him. He was wrong about Rome though. The Rome Luca first knew had emerged from a battlefield saturated in blood, brick-and-mortar temples and palaces rising with the sun to greet the malevolent victor, his father. It had been a paradise on earth, if you were one of the blessed. And he had been, for a long long time – until Sebina's execution fractured his loyalty.

'Nice to see you again, *signore*,' said Thatcher. 'It's been a while. Have you been travelling?'

65

'I've been… recuperating,' said Luca, letting his eyes linger on Thatcher's smiling face.

'What can I get you?' Thatcher's bad Italian translated as 'What is your pleasure?' Luca appreciated that. Desire was a currency he regularly employed in his human transactions. He enjoyed giving pleasure – and taking it away.

'A little information.' Luca squeezed the barista's shoulder. Thatcher started, knocking a cup to the ground. 'The priest with the newspaper. How long has he been coming to the café?'

Thatcher gave a kind of babbling *gah, gah, gah* and then a croak.

'Take your time,' Luca murmured. 'The customers behind me are happy to wait.'

Thatcher mopped his forehead with a towel tucked into the waistband of his jeans. 'For a few days,' he replied, in English.

'The priest? Is he Italian?'

'No idea. Never heard him speak. He's deaf. Signs and reads lips.'

Luca kept his eyes on the young barista. 'Tell me what you've noticed about him.'

'He's always on a laptop, tapping away. Keeps to himself.'

'And?'

Thatcher squirmed. 'He's got a strange tattoo on the inside of his wrist. I've seen it when he picks up his order.'

'Like this?' Luca lifted his T-shirt, exposing a red mark like a brand above his hip, three lines between what looked like parenthesis above and beneath.

Thatcher stared. 'Yeah. Just like that. What is it?'

'It's an ancient musical instrument and my calling.' Luca slipped his hand into the front pocket of his jeans and pulled out a small polished pebble that he handed to Thatcher. 'You've been helpful. Thank you.'

Thatcher rolled the worthless pebble in his hand with a glazed expression on his face. 'Wow. Thanks, man.' He dropped it into the tip jar. 'You want coffee?'

'A double shot.' Luca pointed to a scalloped plate layered with flaky powdered-sugared pastries. 'And *due chiacchiere*.'

'Angel wings,' said Thatcher, smiling. 'Good choice.'

16.

DESPERADO

In a frenzy, Callum yanked the T-shirts and pamphlets from below the counter where he'd hidden the satchel, falling back on his heels with relief when he saw it was still there. Lifting the strap over his head, he hugged it against his chest and came out from behind the counter. If he left now, he'd be late for Signora Orsini, but at least he'd make it.

At the bottom of the stairs, he paused in front of the heavy wooden door. The entire brass plate and handle looked like a cartoon splat, resembling Edvard Munch's famous screaming man. Callum touched his finger curiously to the mass of metal. He thought he could remember it melting, but how was that possible? He felt as if he was coming off ecstasy – hyper-aware and muddled at the same time. Callum swallowed gulps of air, trying to repress his anxiety.

A warm breeze brushed the top of his head. A door slammed upstairs. He had no idea how long he'd been sitting there, but through the small slats of leaded glass at the top of the door, he could see it was still bright outside. Callum stood up. The entryway was small, and he was over six feet. From the second stair up, he kicked hard at the wood above the door's melted lock. Twice. Pain shot up his leg, but the door didn't budge.

His phone pinged. He looked at the text.

Where were you?

Ran into some problems. Need to postpone.

Not happy.

I'll be in touch, I swear.

*

Back upstairs in the library, Callum headed for the butler's pantry and rattled the handle. It was locked. He fished the museum keys out of his pocket. The key got half-way then wouldn't budge. Something was wedged inside the lock.

In a moment of clarity, Callum wondered if someone had deliberately trapped him inside the museum. He ought to have no problem convincing the curator a thief was responsible. After all, some serious flirting and provocative promises were all it had taken to seduce him into trusting Callum with the keys in the first place.

A thief...

He ran into Keats' manuscript room, sliding round the displays, whacking his hip on the sharp edge of a case. He unlocked the lid of the folio case, and with the alarm counting down, flipped open the leather envelope containing Polidori's 'The Fall of the Angels'.

His forgery was gone.

He slammed the case and locked it again, heart hammering. The alarm stopped beeping. Leaning against the glass case, he knew he had a decision to make. Put the original back and all would be well. No one the wiser. Go back to Edinburgh, tail between legs. The months of preparing and the dreams for naught.

Not a chance. He owed that much to Pietra.

Decision made, he ran back into Keats' bedroom, which had the only window in the museum that didn't have bars. Outside, the sun was gilding the Spanish Steps in gold. As Callum pulled his sleeve over his fist and punched through the glass, an alarm screamed. He hauled himself up and out of the window, dangling on the other side for only a second before letting himself drop.

17.

LET'S MAKE A DEAL

Humans in large numbers could be difficult to control. Luca knew this from experience. That was why the First Watcher wanted to open Chaos. He needed a little company to help quell the masses, to build his Second Kingdom.

The agitation among the waiting customers in the café was on the rise. They had jobs to get to. Their rising shuffles and growing murmurs gave Luca a chance to observe the priest folding his newspaper and stepping inside to bus his dishes. He caught the priest's eye for the first time.

'Enjoy your breakfast, Father?' he inquired.

The young man tilted his head, his eyes on Luca's lips. Luca guessed he was no more a priest than Luca was, but in Rome, a cassock and collar gave men a freedom of movement more than any other uniforms, even the police.

In a blur of movement Luca flipped the table in front of the young man, scaring him. The murmurs in the café became screams and shouts. Luca raised a hand.

71

'Quiet,' he said. His voice was calm, his words draping them like a soft blanket. 'Nothing's happening here.'

Slowly, the café settled back into its usual morning routine. Thatcher began taking orders from the queue again. Waiters wound around the upturned table in the centre of the room, delivering coffees and pastries as if it wasn't there.

The priest signed: 'I'm Zach.'

'Ah, you're the Animare.'

The young man's eyes glittered. 'Something like that,' he signed.

Luca nodded. 'So,' he said. 'To business.'

He reached over and dropped the blinds on the window.

18.

A FRIEND OF THE DEVIL

'She has a message for you,' signed Zach.

'Deliver it,' said Luca simply.

Zach's fingers framed the words carefully. 'You've been distracted. The Conjuror has escaped your grasp again. You're spending too much time among humans and it's making you weak.'

Luca's anger crept up his spine, but he shrugged it off. Killing an Animare would be a waste of power that he might need one day. He took in everything about the bold young man before him. His height, his lean build: a good fighter, he thought. His ruffled short blond hair, his emphatic chin. Luca would much rather seduce him than tolerate his disrespect.

'Are those your words or hers?' he said coldly.

'I'm paraphrasing, but she's pissed.'

'She'll recover.' Luca idly picked up the sugar shaker on the next table.

Zach wiped his hands on his cassock and resumed.

'She fears your lack of focus and your continued attempts to take your own revenge on Caravaggio. She wants it to stop. She needs you to focus on the endgame.'

Luca set the sugar shaker ablaze and fast-pitched it at Zach, who ducked. The molten glass and sugar shattered on the wall behind Zach's head. Zach's hand twitched, a pinpoint of light barely visible in his palm.

'There are new orders,' he signed. 'She wants to see you.' Zach's expression was etched with disgust and hate, but for Luca or himself, Luca couldn't tell.

Luca reached across the table, picked Zach up and pinned him like an insect against the wall. His hands slowly tightened.

'You can't kill me,' choked Zach, his neck reddening, his face contorting in pain, his fingers fierce in their movements.

'Your impertinence galls me,' Luca murmured. 'The Camarilla will have another Animare replacing you in an hour. You're not the only one hell-bent on wealth and fame.'

'If you kill me,' mouthed Zach, gasping for air, his hands fighting to loosen the Nephilim's grip, 'you'll never see Sebina again.'

19.

SOMETHING TO BELIEVE IN

'Sebina's *alive*?' The young man's skin blistered under Luca's fingers. 'Impossible. I witnessed her execution.'

Zach choked and gasped.

'You witnessed an animation,' he signed, trying to get away. 'Just an animation. Sebina never climbed into the bull.'

It was too much to believe. To hope. Luca kept pressing. 'Where is she now?'

Zach bicycled his legs frantically. He got his fingers under his cassock and tugged out a gold bloodstone brooch. Held it up for Luca to see. Luca stared. The brooch had belonged to the Duke of Albion, who helped Caravaggio escape from Rome. But Sebina had found it, worn it. Loved it.

'Sebina,' he breathed.

His shock was transforming him slowly from mortal to angel. His wings tugged at his human musculature.

His girth broadened, tearing open his T-shirt, his transformation sucking oxygen from the small café. Thatcher collapsed behind the counter, pulling a tray of pastries on top of his head. Customers lay with their heads on their plates. One of the pastry chefs crawled beneath the swinging door into the kitchen, clawing at his throat.

Luca's wings burst out behind him, filling the small café. He felt Zach's life slipping away beneath his long-tapered fingers. It was sheer force of will that stopped him killing him. Tilting his head back, he exhaled long and slow, sending out a coil of chill breath that spread like a mushroom cloud across the ceiling. Decision made, he let Zach slip to the floor.

In seconds, cool air filled the café again. Customers shifted and groaned. In a swift, elegant movement, Luca's silver-tipped black wings folded into his broad back and vanished, leaving two small stains of blood beneath his shoulder blades.

He helped Thatcher to his feet. Poured two cups of coffee and a glass of iced water, then sorted a plate of pastries before returning to the table. The din in the shop slowly amplified. Business resumed.

Dazed but upright, Zach flopped into a chair.

'What do you want from me?' Luca asked, sipping his coffee.

'It's complicated and dangerous.'

'As am I.'

20.

THE REAL DEAL

Zach walked quickly from the coffee shop to the river where he sat on a bench at a bus stop, rubbing at the blisters on his neck, remembering the terrifying moment when he had been pinned to the café wall, gasping what he believed to be a last breath.

If he was going to survive this mission, he needed to repress his feelings. It had been difficult enough when he'd crossed paths with Em, the only person he'd ever truly loved, in Chicago, and his heart had been broken all over again. But now, so much more was at stake. Not just Em's future. Everyone's.

He'd managed to get under Luca's skin, but could he be trusted to keep his word? Time would tell. No doubt he had pissed Luca off at the coffee shop, pushed him to the edge. But like Luca, Zach's choices were limited too. The risk had to be taken.

It's done.

Zach tapped the words into an encrypted phone. His phone vibrated in his hand.

And?

And we have his attention. He accepted our deal.

Zach closed the phone and returned it to his pocket. Straightening his dusty cassock, he walked towards the Museum of Antiquities on Tiber Island.

21.

SOMEBODY TO LOVE

The young man's deal had stirred something long buried in Luca. Longing, or remembering – or love. The one human emotion he'd allowed to flourish until Sebina had been taken from him. Or perhaps he'd just had too many angel wings, and too much coffee.

He strolled back to his townhouse with its great medieval front door facing the river, unlocked the smaller door cut into its centre and ducked inside. Once a glorious courtyard filled with statues of Roman warriors and a fountain of Oceanus taming the waters of Rome – a fountain that Nicola Salvi had once glimpsed and copied for his iconic Trevi Fountain – the space was now unkempt and overgrown. Thick brush and long weeds reached for sunlight from the cracks and crevices of the paving stones, and wild bougainvillea looked like blood-splattered frescoes against the brick walls.

Down in the cellar, the wooden shelves were depleted of wine and the barrels that had once stood from floor to ceiling full of ale had been drained and repurposed centuries ago. In one arched corner, Luca pressed the palms of his hands against the bricked-up outline of a door. The wall crumbled like chalk under his touch. He dug out the rubble, pleased to see the tiled tunnel was dry. Then he climbed through the hole and hunched his shoulders, walking for a few metres until he was sure the tunnel would lead to the place where it all had begun, and – if the young man was to be trusted – where it would end. Satisfied, he returned to the cellar, where he took apart one of the wine shelves and set the thick planks of wood against the opening.

Back outside, Luca crossed the street. In a moment of hubris, he unfolded his wings and glided down the steps and on to the embankment path on the right bank of the river, where he found a bench and stretched out across it, turning his face to the sky. He'd spent so long in darkness mourning Sebina that the light and space of it seemed an extraordinary thing. His grief was stripped to its essence, but his anger was thicker, harder, more volatile than ever.

Luca's original plan had been to let his father create his Second Kingdom and then destroy it at a time of his own choosing, make him and his followers pay for killing Sebina. It would be amusing, to see the humans scuttle about the Watchers like obedient rats, and even more amusing to see his father's reaction at such a betrayal so late in the day. But this new arrangement was giving him pause. Perhaps the Camarilla wasn't as watertight as they thought. And Sebina...

It seemed there was a better way after all.

A homeless woman on the grassy knoll above the path gave Luca the stink eye, spitting a ream of angry words at him, holding her fingers in a sign of the cross. Ah, she'd seen his wings. Luca ignored her, focusing on the implications of what he'd learned, what he was being asked to do.

The river was empty of any traffic, flowing fast around the curve before it split into two tributaries around Tiber Island. The last time Luca had held Sebina, it had been on the river not far from this spot. The night Caravaggio had escaped their clutches, the night Luca should have torn the bastard into pieces instead of leaving him to drown in the rat-infested shallows.

Nearby, the homeless woman was reciting the rosary, tiny beads flitting through her fingers like sand. It amused Luca when humans spotted him and believed he was evil. He was, if anything, open to all options. That was the beauty of him.

Clasping his hands behind his head, he stared at the white-hot sun in the shockingly blue sky. An Airbus 380 banked overhead in preparation for its final descent into Leonardo da Vinci – Fiumicino Airport. Luca was fascinated with aircraft of all shapes and sizes, the bigger the better. Their power intoxicated him. Their aesthetic thrilled him.

He smiled at the white fumes brushing across the blue. In his divine form, his presence left the same marks on the atmosphere. In centuries past, his contrails had raised concern, even sparked a little crazy among those who spotted them, but thanks to the Wright brothers and Boeing, these days Luca could fly over the world almost in plain sight.

The homeless woman stirred herself and trundled away, spitting on the silver-capped toes of his boots. Luca instinctively raised his hand to set her possessions on fire, but then changed his mind. *Love*, he thought. The feeling was familiar, but alien at the same time. A complicated emotion.

Absently, he rained a handful of coins into the homeless woman's cart. She let out a terrified yelp and scuttled away. He sat up and wiped her phlegm from his boot.

22.

POSSESSION

Cecilia Ciardi stood on the terrace of the Garden of Oranges on the Aventine Hill, inhaling the spectacular view from one of Rome's highest vantage points. She had visited the garden every morning since her return to the city a week ago. Behind her stood the remains of a rectangular stone edifice, the Temple of Juno. The famous hills of Rome stretched ahead, the panorama breath-taking. On the Palatine Hill, the ruins of the Forum were like bones bursting through the lush green ground. Cecilia extended her arms towards the city as if accepting its laurels and accolades.

She checked her Bulgari with the simple mother-of-pearl face and brown strap in which she'd punched an extra hole. Her grandfather had always said the watch was like her: steadfast, resilient, beautiful – an Italian classic. She was late for a board meeting to discuss the weekend's gala. She thought about calling her driver and having him bring the car round, but changed her mind. Hiking up her white linen maxi dress, she retrieved a leather portfolio and her handbag from the bench and walked briskly downhill towards the river and the Museum of Antiquities on Tiber Island, where she kept her offices.

The streets were crowded with happy worshippers heading towards St Peter's Square for an open-air mass. She threaded through the crowd with a smile in her eyes and a song on her lips. She couldn't remember the last time she'd felt the warm sun on her face and a light summer breeze on her legs. She almost skipped.

Until recently, Cecilia had had a successful career as a fashion model. But on hearing of her grandfather's death, she'd walked off a runway in Paris and disappeared for two months. The press had a feeding frenzy on the crumbs of information her inner circle dropped for them. She was in mourning. She was taking over the family business. She was on a pilgrimage. She was healing. She was, and she was.

When she returned to Rome, her inner circle saw a changed woman. Healthier, with more gravitas, but more ambitious too. Two nights earlier, she had announced from the portico of the Museum of Antiquities that her family's sacred artefacts from centuries of collecting would go on display for the first time ever, the opening to be celebrated with a spectacular concert performance of 'Black Orpheus' two days from now in St Peter's Square. The announcement had caused a sensation not only because secular concerts in the sacred square were rare, but also rumours were swirling that a world-famous performer was coming out of retirement to play Eurydice. Every media outlet, online and old school, scheduled to stream it.

Cecilia was midway across the Ponte Garibaldi when a white Transit van seemed to speed deliberately towards her. A blue Vespa shot out from behind the van, sending it swerving into oncoming traffic. Brakes screeched. Horns blared. The Vespa veered in front of a trundling bus, jumped up on to the curb and skidded to a halt in front of Cecilia.

Every person on the bridge went into flight mode, apart from Cecilia, who fell back against the wall, clutching the portfolio close. The traffic sped up, carrying vehicles as fast as the two narrow lanes allowed. A few passengers hung out of windows, fists raised. Regaining control, the Transit van shot the lights at the far end of the bridge and disappeared.

The Vespa driver shut off her bike and raised her hands apologetically in the air. 'Sorry! Sorry! Sorry!' She took off her helmet, her short blonde hair plastered against her head. Dressed in a flowery sundress and calf-high biker boots, she clasped her hands in front of her face apologetically.

'I thought they were going to get you,' she said. 'Are you hurt?'

Cecilia blinked a couple of times against the setting sun. 'I'm fine,' she finally said in English, wincing from a pain shooting from her ankle to her knee.

'They looked like they were going to run you down. Do you need a lift?'

Cecilia brushed off her dress, then looked to the end of the bridge. The van was long gone.

'*Grazie*, Sol,' she said. 'I accept your offer of a ride.'

Sol passed her helmet to Cecilia and insisted she wear it. Cecilia tucked the portfolio under her arm and then wrapped her thin arms round Sol's waist, caressing a piece of her dress fabric between her fingers. 'Prada?'

'Si.'

'*Molto bella.*'

Sol bounced the scooter over the curb, shooting it like a missile back into traffic. A passing wing mirror smacked against Cecilia's arm as Sol made a U-turn into the opposite lane, barely avoiding another head-on collision. She turned south at high speed on to the Lungotevere de' Cenci, forgetting that at this part of the city traffic ran north. Rows of traffic hurtled towards them, blasting away like cavalry at war.

'Oh shit. Hold on!'

Cecilia tightened her grip. 'One piece, Sol,' she said. 'I need to get there in one piece!'

Sol shifted gears and prepared to cut on to the grassy verge when suddenly – inexplicably – the traffic parted like the Red Sea. Sol shot down the middle. At the next intersection, the same thing happened, allowing Sol to navigate the Vespa back towards the island.

Cecilia leaned close to Sol's ear. 'I think you've got a bit of the devil in you.'

23.

OUT OF TIME

Twenty minutes later, Cecilia marched irritably along a line of sculpted hedges and blossoming bougainvillea framing the grounds of the museum, adjusting the leather portfolio under her arm. Her dress was torn at the bottom where her hem had snagged on the scooter's kick-stand, serving to worsen her mood. The Museum of Antiquities was housed in the Castello Caetani on the west side of Tiber Island, a landmass shaped like a ship in the middle of the river. The island had protected Roman citizens when their city was under siege from war and from plagues. Her knee was twingeing, but not enough to worry about. The pain reminded her she was alive.

Her private rooms had tall rectangular windows on three sides. Like a series of altar panels, the windows were positioned precisely to display the ruins of the Forum, the magnificent Arch of Constantine and the external bones of the Colosseum. Modern Rome was cut off, outside the frames of the windows.

Cecilia ducked slightly beneath a stone temple arch incorporated into the door – she was considerably taller than her female ancestors – and tossed the portfolio on her desk. The suite was furnished like a salon with a cluster of grey and cream Nutuzzi chairs like giant cupped hands in front of a modern glass desk. Low shelf units in black Cyprus crisscrossed the room. Roman statues of Jupiter, Minerva and Mars stood facing each other from different corners in the room; each one thought to have been destroyed centuries ago.

Cecilia had designed the space to resemble a gallery tucked inside an Italian villa, and she'd succeeded. Every artefact, bust, statue and reliquary from her family's collection had been positioned with care by her own hands; hands which she now clasped in front of her. She beckoned with a tilt of her head the two men in black suits and crisp white shirts waiting on the other side of the room.

'Someone tried to kill me this afternoon,' she told them. 'On the bridge. A white van. In *my* town. The nerve of it defies belief.'

'We know,' said the older of the two men. 'Sol has already informed us.'

His eyes were bloodshot and he'd been biting the skin around his fingernails while he waited. He *should* be nervous, Cecilia thought. He should be terrified.

The younger man cleared his throat. Cecilia smiled at him. He had been recommended by Sol who she trusted more than anyone else in her life at this moment. Corralling Luca Ferrante, giving him her message; that had not been an easy thing to do.

Zach Butler was quickly making himself indispensable. Uninvolved and unattainable, his bold choice of celibacy had initially raised her suspicions, but Zach was a technological wizard, and Cecilia appreciated the ways he had updated her network and tightened the security on the museum's treasures. His body was lithe and lean, his good looks underscored with a simmering anger. She liked that about him too. Anger was much more malleable than acceptance.

The older man held his hands in front of his chest like a penitent about to take communion.

'Are you sure you want to pursue this path before the concert?' he asked. 'It seems needlessly risky. Why call attention to us more than necessary?'

'Are you questioning my authority, Victor?'

'Of course not,' Victor Moretti said, bowing his head. 'It's just that I fear—'

'What do you fear?' Cecilia inquired, stepping closer to him. 'That the Camarilla have not made you rich enough? That we have not given you enough power? That your children have not visited enough countries yet?'

Victor blanched. Cecilia smiled.

'I know you've sent your family from Rome,' she said. 'Tut tut, Victor. Just when we need you most.'

'They needed a break from this summer heat,' he said, a whimper catching his words.

Cecilia tipped her head to one side. 'You and your family have always been weak. For centuries, you have managed to avoid the real work that has to be done. My grandfather tolerated it because he adored your mother, but I have no such feelings for her, or for you.'

Zach laid out a carafe of wine and two silver goblets on a nearby table then stepped away. Cecilia poured wine into each one, wiping the excess from the lip of the carafe with one of the white linen napkins sitting on the tray. The red wine stained the monogram of the Camarilla like a bloody kiss. She handed the glass to Victor. With trembling hands, he accepted, bowed his head and backed away from the table, but he didn't take a drink.

Footsteps echoed across the floor from the stairs. Victor looked over at the figure who'd entered and what was in their hands.

He dropped to his knees and spread himself in front of Cecilia in full supplication, his goblet clattering across the floor, the wine puddling at his feet.

'Please,' he begged, choking back a sob. 'I can be stronger. I can do better.' He lifted his eyes to the new arrival and then back to Cecilia. 'You need me.'

'Not any more.'

24.

EVERYTHING'S TRUE BUT
EVERYTHING LIES

'Stay,' Cecilia instructed Victor when he tried to get to his knees. She put her foot on his head and pressed his face into the travertine. 'I'm not interested in your failures any more.'

She increased the pressure on his skull with her foot. A bone in his jaw cracked. He cried out, blood flowing from his nose.

'I promise to leave your family alone if...' Cecilia paused, lifted her foot a little, relieving some of the pressure. 'If, and only if, you answer my question with the honesty the cause deserves.'

'Yes, yes!'

She crouched down. Victor remained prostrate, a puddle spreading out beneath his trousers.

'Who else does Orion have spying on us?' she asked softly.

The person who had entered the room raised a broad

sword above Victor's head. Cecilia took the sword from Sol.

'Who?' she repeated, weighing the sword.

'No one, no one!' Victor sobbed. He tried to lift his head. 'It's the truth.'

Cecilia cracked his jawbone against the marble again.

'No one, I swear!' His words slid out with a bloody, broken tooth.

Cecilia's fury shook the room. She raised the sword and brought it down on Victor's neck with such force that the blade cracked the travertine, sending sparks into the air.

'Thank you, Sol,' said Cecilia, returning the sword. 'You've been helpful today.'

Sol bowed her head. 'I have someone checking all the street cameras for the white van,' she said. 'I think we'll find it was someone working on behalf of Victor himself.'

'Orion,' said Cecilia. Her voice dripped with scorn. 'Hoping to avoid losing Victor if they killed me first. As if they could.'

'Now that Victor is out of the way,' said Sol, 'may we proceed as planned?'

Cecilia's grim expression relaxed a little. 'The lyre is within our reach. The Devil's Interval too. And someone I trust is watching the Conjuror. So yes. We are almost ready.'

Sol stepped over the pool of blood. 'I'll have this cleaned up.'

'Wait.' Cecilia picked up Victor's head by its hair. She set it on the silver tray, using her napkin to dab blood from its mouth. 'Let's get a picture of this. I'm sure his wife would like an update on her husband's whereabouts.'

'What about Luca?' Sol asked. 'Can we depend on him to exterminate the Order of Era Mina? Take out the vaults?'

'Zach gave him the message,' said Cecilia. 'The Nephilim will bend to our will.'

Sol used Victor's jacket to wipe his blood from the sword blade. Cecilia drew her close and kissed her on the lips.

'Your service will not go unrewarded,' she said. 'But first, I need you to fetch something the Scottish student has stolen.'

'The student who was working with Pietra Scoretti? Callum Muir?'

'Yes. I paid him a visit earlier today. I thought he knew nothing of Pietra's plans. I showed him mercy and left him with his life. But I was misinformed.' Cecilia picked up the portfolio from her desk and flipped it open. 'This map is a forgery.'

'How can you be sure?'

'It's lifeless.' Cecilia cast it back on to the desk in disgust. 'Dull. The real map is still out in the world. It cannot fall into Orion's hands before the concert. Not when everything else we need is within our grasp.'

Sol ran a hand through her blonde hair. 'You want another accident? Like Pietra's?'

Cecilia squeezed Sol's arm and dropped a set of keys into her hand. 'I took these from the boy earlier. Be as creative as you like. But get me that original.'

A few minutes later, with Victor's head on its silver platter, Sol headed into the labyrinth of tunnels and catacombs that stretched beneath the original foundations of the island, all the way to Vatican City.

25.

WHAT'S YOUR NAME?

Sol had just left the building when Luca strolled through the lobby of the Museum of Antiquities, ignoring the plinths and pedestals displaying busts of men and women he'd once known inhabiting the space. He was about to head up the wide stairs to the Camarilla's private offices when an icy breeze checked him. He cautiously followed the sweet scent of oranges below the stairs to the museum's archives.

If he was surprised by what he found, he had enough sense not to show it.

Cecilia's stilettos floated centimetres off the ground as she reached a high shelf stacked with scrolls. She arched a brow at Luca's entrance.

'Good of you to grace us with your presence.'

'Are you a believer?' asked Luca, more insolently than was wise. His human emotions were a toxic blend.

'Always the defiant one.' She grasped a scroll tied with a red band and floated back to the ground.

Luca bowed slightly before adding in a more controlled tone, 'What should I call you now, your Eminence? Father seems a little... inaccurate.'

'Cecilia.' She smoothed her hands thoughtfully down the length of the body-hugging dress. 'She has given me a new outlook on this world.'

'Is that why you've summoned me?'

'I've summoned you because I need you to take care of something,' she said. 'Try not to fail... again. The time is upon us. We must raise the Second Kingdom.'

Luca shoved his hands in his jeans and scanned the room. It was as he remembered it from four hundred years earlier, with the exception of the top-of-the-line security system and the controlled air, and the alcove full of glowing musical instruments stolen over the centuries from Animare paintings – evidence of the Camarilla's failed attempts to find the lyre. Leather-bound over-sized volumes to tiny pocket-sized books filled the shelves. Frescoes covered the vaulted ceiling with images of god and goddess, and apothecary jars filled with plant and human matter stocked surrounding cabinets. The room was rich with the musk of dark magic and the power of ancient manuscripts.

Cecilia loosened the band and unrolled the scroll. Luca stiffened. He recognized it as one that had been hidden in the Tomb of Martyrs. It had disappeared during his last confrontation with the Conjuror. He'd assumed it had fallen into the hands of whoever was protecting the

Conjuror. How did it get here? Was an Orion agent working both sides?

'Where did you get that?'

'One of my generals brought it to me as a token of loyalty. He felt he had something to prove.' Cecilia eyed Luca. 'As do you.'

Luca bowed ironically. 'What is it that you wish me to do?'

Cecilia brushed a fleck of dust from her dress. 'Since my re-awakening, I've learned that the Camarilla have been taking musical instruments from paintings, in a fruitless bid to find the lyre.' She flicked her hand dismissively at the glowing objects in the alcove. 'We both know they could have simply asked you where it was.'

A sudden pain stabbed Luca's skull. A trickle of blood splashed like a tear from the corner of his eye on to the scroll in Cecilia's hands.

'You were once the best of us, Luca.' Cecilia traced a finger over the blood spatter and slowly raised it to her lips. 'Until you allowed yourself to love. You must subvert your human nature or Orion will destroy you with their lies.'

She pressed her hand on top of Luca's. A hot vice squeezed his brain. He was burning up inside.

'You are my offspring, anointed in fire to be my general. When the others rise, I want you by my side.'

The fire in Luca's brain subsided. Cecilia smiled. 'But first, prove that you are loyal... to me alone.'

Blood and darkness and destiny bound Luca to this being, this Watcher. But was it enough any more? An image of Sebina flashed across his mind.

Cecilia's expression darkened. 'Do not fail me. Bring down the Order of Era Mina, and bring me the lyre.'

26.

CLOSED FOR REPAIR

Callum landed on a group of teenagers slouching, drinking and smoking on the broad steps directly beneath the museum's window. He untangled himself, and while they screamed their wrath in English and Italian, he sprinted to the top of the Spanish Steps behind the obelisk in front of the Trinity dei Monti. He stopped at the portico and looked back down at the Spanish Steps.

Police had started to gather under the window, and the teenagers swiftly moved on. Several Fiat squad cars blasted up to the museum, and the area was cordoned off. One or two armed soldiers sprinted across the square. Their presence ramped up the situation at once.

Callum ducked inside the church where he found an open pew near the back, his heart racing, his mind flipping through his options. He scanned his surroundings. All the church signs were in French, then Italian and finally English, the largest announcing that the pipe organ was under repair until further notice.

Callum had jacked his hip on someone's shoulder when he'd dropped from the window. It was sore to the touch. He cautiously stretched his legs out across the wooden bench, folded his hands over the satchel and wondered what the hell he was going to do.

'Excuse me?'

An Englishman wearing a blue windbreaker was poking gently at Callum's shoulder. 'Do you mind moving over?' He pointed to his wife and two teenage sons standing in the aisle.

Callum sat up with a start. The nave was filling up and the gates to the high altar were open. Around him, a steady stream of worshippers was entering the church for the evening mass. Mumbling something about leaving, he slid along the pew and out into the main aisle. The family watched him curiously before they settled themselves.

Callum's head was in a fog, but he knew two things for sure. He needed to get his head straight, and he had to hide the illustration. The curator would be on to him at once.

He glanced around for a place to hide his satchel. The church was more austere than most, lacking in grottos and side chapels, with only a handful of effigies and a small chorus of statues. It was better known for its frescoes of the Old and New Testament, and its massive pipe organ.

The organ. Callum remembered the construction notice. He moved among a flock of worshippers towards the high altar, darting through the wrought iron gate. Then he dropped back into the shadows, and waited until he was sure he was alone. The moment the coast was clear, he slipped next to the organ, crawled under the construction tape, and tucked the satchel with his treasure beneath the decorative console and a wide pedalboard.

27.

WANTED FOR QUESTIONING

Rome at night always seemed more muted to Callum than Edinburgh or Glasgow. Whereas all three cities had vibrant nightlives, there was something about the light here, the way it slanted off the monuments, the way it washed through the shadows on the narrow streets, the way it rained from the moonlight.

Yawning from his afternoon nap, he left the church and worked his way to the closest metro heading south to San Lorenzo. Standing on the platform, he caught a flash of his name on a digital news tracker, scrolling above the track.

Son of British Lord, Sir Archibald Muir, wanted for questioning in connection with murder of Rome banker, Victor Moretti, whose headless body was found earlier today floating in the Tiber.

A rush of disgorging travellers jostled Callum as he stood in shock, watching his passport photo scroll across the screen. He sprang to life, squeezing on to the train at the last second, head down, riding the seven stops into San Lorenzo. Thinking harder than he'd ever thought in his life.

He felt sure the police would be watching the garret where he had lived with Pietra. Callum decided instead to head to his flat, a couple of rooms he'd hardly used since arriving in Rome. Even though it stretched his funds every month, Callum had hung on to the flat as well as helping Pietra to pay for the garret. It had essentially become a place to store his crap that Pietra didn't want.

The flat was only a block from the garret, but keeping to the dimly lit streets and the crowded alleys, the journey took him longer than he'd hoped. It wasn't until he reached the building that he realized he'd lost his keys. When he tried to remember where he'd last seen them, his memory grew foggy again.

He sat inside the doorway to the building and tried to make sense of why he was wanted for the murder of an Italian banker. If he hadn't been so scared and confused, the irony might have been funny. He'd had no money in a bank since he'd left Scotland. He was about to contemplate breaking in when a tall lanky figure found him tucked against the wall.

'Jesus, Callum. You scared me!' Raoul was carrying groceries shoved inside his book bag, a bunch of leafy carrots poking out the top. A friend of Pietra's, he was studying at the university and had found this flat for

Callum in the first place. 'You look like you've been hit by a bus.'

'By a set of stone steps and a pile of teenagers, actually,' Callum said.

Raoul pushed open the outside door and waited until Callum hobbled into a hallway that reeked of overflowing rubbish from cans lining the interior wall. 'Are you hurt badly?'

'Just banged up,' said Callum. 'Do you still have my spare key?'

Ten minutes later Callum was in his shower, his clothes in a heap in the middle of the floor, the hot water running over him. He pressed his forehead on the chipped tiles.

What the hell was going on?

Pietra would have had answers. He pulled the curtain closed and sat in the tub, wishing the last month had never happened. He began to shiver, pulled himself up, his hip aching from his jump out of the window. Then he grabbed a towel and walked into a bedroom the size of his closet in Edinburgh.

From the street below he heard a car door slam and loud Italian voices. He moved cautiously to the window. His view of the rooftops was one of the reasons he'd loved this place when he first arrived, and dozens of pencil sketches in the light of dawn, the brilliance of high noon and the soft shadows of dusk layered the walls around the window. The view was also how he and Pietra had discovered their garret; its skylights shimmered opposite the flat like pools of water. His grief took his breath away as he stared across the roofs.

He glimpsed movement.

Reaching for the binoculars he kept on the window ledge, he adjusted them to focus on the garret windows. His whole body stiffened at the grotesque tableau.

No way was he getting out of this situation without some *serious* help.

28.

STILL LIFE WITH BANKER

A severed head lay on a silver tray with a white cloth draped around the edges. Mouth wide open, empty eyes staring. The head was as horrible as in Caravaggio's famous painting. Callum dropped the binoculars against his chest and backed away from the window. The banker. Had to be.

He forced himself to look again. The space was chaos, clothes and books strewn everywhere. Pietra's favourite Frida Kahlo tapestry had been torn from the wall. All of his art supplies and chemicals were in disarray next to the sink, his light table smashed and his inks spilled. The wardrobe had been moved closer to the door and the couch had been pulled away from the slope of the ceiling. And down in the street, the police were watching, waiting for his return.

Callum dropped the binoculars, pulled on his boots and slipped his phone under the waistband of his jeans. Thinking better of it – they might be able to trace him

– he ground the phone under the heel of his boot, then dropped it into the sink and ran the water.

Scrambling into the tub, Callum punched open the narrow bathroom window and climbed outside on to the flat roof. Ducking low, he ran to the other side of the building where he flattened himself in the shadows of the roof air vents before scrambling on to the fire escape at the back of the building, unhooking the mechanism and sliding to the ground with a bone-shaking clatter.

Raoul flung open his kitchen window as Callum hurtled past.

'What the hell's going on?' he yelled down the building.

'You never saw me, man.' Callum jumped off the fire escape and on to the ground, his hip throbbing.

He heard the window slam as he jogged into the alley between the apartment building and a restaurant. The smartest option would be to cut his losses and get out of Rome. At the very least find a haven where he could figure out why all of this was happening. But Callum was so bloody angry that neither of these options appealed. He was going to see this through for Pietra's sake.

Staying close to the shadows as the sun went down, he headed towards the Tiber, determined to do two things. Talk to Fiera Orsini. Stay alive.

29.

TAKE THE CANNOLI

Any night in the summer, the cobbled alleys and narrow streets of the Trastevere were packed with revellers. He would be safer there. Callum kept to alleys and crowded squares, feeling reasonably sure he hadn't been followed. When he made it safely on to the Ponte Sisto, he slowed, catching his breath, figuring out a plan of sorts. Time to take advantage of the good nature and hospitality of Rome's citizenry.

Crossing into Trastevere, he stopped at the first off-licence he came across and bought a magnum of prosecco and a sleeve of plastic cups. Then he tucked the cups and the prosecco under his arm and headed along the narrow street towards the Piazza Santa Maria.

Callum stopped in front of a bar and its crowded patio. He held up the bottle and glasses. 'It's my birthday,' he announced. 'Girlfriend just dumped me. Who wants a drink?'

Well-wishers crowded around him, cheerful and drunken.

'Her loss.'

'Happy Birthday.'

'Pour me one!'

'If you need a shoulder to cry on, mine's available.'

Taking advantage of the pressing crowd, Callum took the first opportunity to escape around the side of the bar, his back to the wall, keeping to the shadows. No one was looking. No one had followed.

As he had expected, *La Madrina* was holding court at the front table of her restaurant. Callum watched as neighbours, friends, business owners, and any number of sycophants stopped at the table to give Signora Orsini her tithes: everything from flowers to wine to small wrapped packages that Callum knew held payment for keeping the area safe and profitable. There was nothing legal or illegal that happened in Trastevere that she didn't know about. She'd already paid for half of the original illustration upfront. If she still wanted it as badly as he thought she did, then she might also be willing to help him.

A waiter poured cognac, and waited for Signora Orsini to nod her approval before he moved on. She lifted the glass to her bright red lips, taking a sip before setting the glass down and using the inside of her thumb to erase her lip-print.

According to Pietra, cognac was always *La Madrina*'s last drink of the night. If he was going to confront her, it had to be soon. In public, she'd be less likely to kill him right away for missing their earlier meeting. Whereas in private... Word would have reached her by now of the warrant for his arrest, and she might want to make an example of him. He thought of the banker's head, and shivered.

He slid down the wall and rested his arms on his legs, closing his eyes. How the hell had he got here?

When he looked up, *La Madrina* was staring down at him. She carried little excess on her thin body. Two rugged young men in a uniform of black trousers and white shirts flanked her. The alley was suddenly deserted.

'My dear young Englishman,' she said.

'Scottish,' he said without thinking.

She chopped the silver knob of her cane across his shins. 'Bring him.'

Callum winced from the pain as he was yanked to his feet. For better or worse, some dilemmas resolved themselves.

30.

STEALTH MODE

When one of the bodyguards clicked open the trunk of the black Mercedes, Callum shielded his eyes from the bright lights while doing his best to climb out of the trunk with grace.

He gazed with awe at the mansion peeking out from a tree-covered hillside on a curve of the Tiber. He'd read about the place, how the Vatican had once housed a stream of ever-changing mistresses of cardinals and popes here, before the title and land had transferred to the Orsini family to pay off a pope's gambling debt. The Orsinis had held it as their seat of power ever since. He noted the arched ruins of a bridge designed by Michelangelo with particular interest. It was unfinished, but the original plan had been to connect the Villa Orsini with another palace of similar repute on the other side of the Tiber.

Signora Fiera Orsini was already out of sight. Callum followed the guard into the loggia of the palace, gripping the satchel. He couldn't stop himself from gasping. The astonishing fresco began at one side of the massive mahogany front doors, circling around the walls beneath a wide marble staircase where Romulus and Remus fought each other for the city of Rome, and ended with Romulus' victory. Other artists had painted myths on the borders of the ceiling. The dome above the stairs reminded Callum of Botticelli's *Birth of Venus*, except the figure was male and was rising from the earth inside a ring of fire rather than the sea. He couldn't tear his eyes away.

'Breathtaking, I know.' *La Madrina* had appeared beside him. 'The dome was painted when Lorenzo de'Medici owned the palace. It's the only Botticelli outside the Vatican that doesn't belong to the Uffizi.'

It *was* Botticelli then, thought Callum, feeling dazed. 'And the Roman fresco is Raphael?'

'Most of it,' she said. 'The rest was completed by his students.'

She tapped her cane on the marble floor. Another attractive young Italian appeared in seconds at her side. 'We'll have supper in my salon, Andrea. Set a place for my guest. This way, young man,' she said, beckoning Callum. 'We have a lot to discuss.'

Callum followed her along a hallway to an old-fashioned lift in the shape of a birdcage. It didn't look big enough for two. Signora Orsini used her cane to tap a gold button and stepped inside.

'Bring Signore Muir to my salon, Enzo,' she murmured to a guard as the golden doors closed.

Callum turned to see another chiselled servant waiting for him. Perhaps, to work for *La Madrina*, you needed a stealth mode.

31.

A LONG DAY'S JOURNEY
INTO NIGHT

The salon was on the third floor, tucked in the northwest corner of the palace. Comfortably furnished, the room was modest in size with an unlit fireplace, a wall of built-in bookcases, and four tall windows looking out over the treetops towards the floodlit Vatican.

Callum stood hesitantly at the doorway until Andrea had finished setting supper out for each of them on a round coffee table.

'Sit. Eat,' Signora Orsini instructed. 'Then we will talk.'

Callum thought he'd lost his appetite after seeing the grotesque display in the garret, but he ate the plate of cheeses and meats quickly enough, saving the two *arancini* – tiny fried balls of rice and cheese – for last.

La Madrina was watching him closely. He wondered if he could make a run for the windows and jump into the gardens if things got out of hand.

'Relax,' she said. 'If I were going to hurt you, I would

already have done so.' She dabbed her lips with her napkin and stood. At an open bar on a shelf of the bookcase, she poured a glass of port from a crystal decanter. 'May I offer you something other than water?'

Callum would have liked nothing more than to drink away the entire nightmare of the past month, but he shook his head and sat back in the chair, his hands resting on its over-stuffed arms, his adrenaline dissipating.

'Pietra was a loss to all of us,' Signora Orsini said, unexpectedly. 'I've known her family for years. I fear they'll never recover. I'm sorry.'

Callum squeezed the arms of the chair, pressing back his grief. 'Thank you.'

'Still, you missed our appointment.'

'I couldn't get away,' Callum blurted. 'Something strange happened at the museum and I was locked inside.' In a rush, he told her about the door and the strange woman. 'I thought maybe she was working for you. Did you plan to take the original and cut me out?'

Her tone stiffened. 'I would not have done that. I gave Pietra my word.'

Callum's full stomach and overwhelming exhaustion were making it difficult to keep his eyes open. 'I think the woman in the museum may have drugged or hypnotized me. Whoever she works for is going to be really pissed off when they realize she took a forgery.'

'My thoughts exactly. That's why I think you've been framed for Victor Moretti's murder and it's why I've brought you here.' She finished her port and set it on the table.

Relief washed over Callum in a flood. 'I never met the man.'

Signora Orsini gestured at Callum's empty hands with her cane. 'I can see that you don't have the original illustration with you.'

He shook his head. 'I hid it until I could figure out what was happening.'

'I can help you with that.'

Again, she tapped her cane, this time on the hardwood floor. Andrea appeared.

'Signora?'

'Coffee, Andrea.' As *La Madrina* looked at Callum, he thought he saw a flash of fear in her eyes. 'It may be a long night.'

32.

HEAVEN IS A PLACE ON EARTH

'Like all efficient secret societies, the Camarilla's beginnings are clouded in conspiracy and mystery,' said Signora Orsini. 'They were formed as an elite legion to protect the first King of Rome. When Romulus died, they continued to protect his descendants.'

'Like a family's private army?'

The older woman inclined her head. 'If both family and army consisted of supernatural beings, yes.'

Callum swallowed too quickly, the coffee catching in his throat. 'You're not serious,' he said, coughing.

La Madrina looked coolly at him. She wasn't the sort of woman to fool around. Callum reminded himself that he'd seen a door melt, a woman vanish from a locked room, and a head on a platter in his flat. Nothing was normal or natural in his life any more.

Signora Orsini set her cup and saucer on the table, walked over to one of the bookshelves where she ran her fingers along their spines until she found what she was looking for. She pulled out the book and handed it to Callum. The title was printed in raised gold letters: *Book of Songs*.

Callum opened it.

'A true compendium of conjurations, invocations, curses, and the mystical instruments to raise up the Watchers and bring the Second Kingdom to earth,' he read aloud. 'What are Watchers?'

'Fallen angels,' said Signora Orsini. 'Trapped in Chaos. For now.'

'Angels,' said Callum, carefully. 'Right.'

On the next page of the ancient book was a tree similar to the illustration he'd forged. But instead of rising out of the ground with strange glyphs on each of its branches, this tree was spread across the pages with the trunk at the centre, its roots spreading under what Callum knew was an ancient world-view: every land mass connected and birthed from what was labelled as the Tree of Life. He looked up.

'It looks like Byron's tree,' he said. 'But here it's more like a world map.'

'It is indeed a map,' said Signora Orsini. 'A map stolen from the Camarilla centuries ago. It is, needless to say, by neither Byron nor Polidori. Polidori's papers were simply a convenient place to hide it.'

The headache that was tapping at the edge of Callum's brain was thumping now. The shot of caffeine hadn't helped. Neither had the food.

'The Camarilla knew that Pietra had discovered the map,' said Signora Orsini. 'But they did not know of your plan to forge a duplicate. They are now hunting for you. They can't afford to have a copy muddying the waters before they implement their final plan.'

Callum wanted to believe he was experiencing some kind of grief-stricken hallucination, but the elegant woman sipping coffee in front of him was all too real.

'How do you know all of this?'

'My great-grandmother was Francis Polidori's sister,' the older woman continued. 'She realized that he had discovered the map, and it had resulted in his murder.'

Callum set down his cup. 'I thought Polidori committed suicide because his poem was badly received?'

'That's the story they let circulate. It made everything easier.'

'So the illustration is a map,' Callum repeated, trying to get his head around what the older woman was telling him. 'A map to what?'

'The map depicts the place where a Conjuror is prophesied to open the portal to Chaos.' Callum noticed the fearful look in Signora Orsini's eyes again. 'When the portal is opened, the Watchers will rise and make slaves of us all in their Second Kingdom.'

'What was the first one?' Not sure what else to say.

'It's had many names. Paradise, Elysium, Olympus – a place of the divine before time was measured.'

A jumble of questions ricocheted around Callum's head. But before he'd had a chance to ask any of them, Andrea burst into the room, breathless and pale.

'He's here,' he gasped.

Callum jumped to his feet, knocking his shin against the coffee table. 'Should I be worried?'

La Madrina moved with surprising agility to the door. 'I thought we'd have more time. You are connected to Victor Moretti, you see, and the Camarilla are exploiting that connection.'

'I swear I never met the man!' Callum protested.

'He arranged the money for me to buy the illustration. There is your connection. Now, there's someone you must meet if you are going to survive.'

33.

REVELATIONS

A young man was staring up at the domed ceiling with his hands folded behind his back, the long tails of his vintage tuxedo not quite hiding a leather sketchpad with a pen clipped to its cover. He looked as if he'd stepped out of an Italian opera. Straight blond hair slicked back with product, an old-fashioned wing-collared white shirt, an untied bow tie. His eyes were the most unusual colour of blue, like aggies: big blue marbles. He nodded at Callum.

'You're here already,' said Signora Orsini dryly. 'That can't be good. Have you been at the opera? You look quite dashing.'

Callum watched as the young man moved his hands fluidly through the air. Sign language.

'Dinner at the Vatican?' said *La Madrina*. 'What did Cecilia want you to do there? Never mind, tell me later. Ah, she's personally invited the Pope to her concert.' She turned to Callum. 'Callum, this is Zach Butler. He is also from Scotland. Among other amazing abilities, he reads lips exceptionally well.'

Zach's handshake was warm and firm.

With her hand on Callum's arm, Signora Orsini nudged Zach towards a salon to the right of the front doors. 'Zach, I need you to get Callum out of Rome tonight.'

Callum pulled away. 'Woah! I'm not leaving,' he protested. 'Whatever's going on, I'm going to see it through.'

Zach's face was sympathetic as he moved his hands.

'We can't bring Pietra back,' said Signora Orsini, squeezing Callum's arm. 'We did what we could, but we were too late.'

Callum froze. 'What about Pietra?'

'I am so sorry,' she said simply.

Callum backed up to the bottom stair, shaking his head. He'd probably known since early this afternoon that Pietra's death hadn't been an accident. Best laid plans get really effed up.

Signora Orsini placed a slim hand on his shoulder. 'She didn't suffer. Zach was watching you both from the moment you came to my restaurant and took that money. The map was too important to risk.'

Callum felt a great weight pressing down on him. Zach tried to catch him before he collapsed, but he shoved him away and slumped against the wall. His stomach was pitching madly and he thought he might be sick.

'I liked Pietra,' said Signora Orsini gently. 'Truly.'

'The Camarilla wanted the sketch enough to murder Pietra for it,' whispered Callum. 'Didn't they?'

'They've murdered for much less,' said Signora Orsini matter-of-factly.

Callum wanted to howl. He wanted to hit someone. 'This is all my fault. If I hadn't been so bloody arrogant to think we could live without my trust fund, she'd still be alive! Who was it? Give me a name, dammit!'

'Who knows? A mercenary,' said Signora Orsini. 'Someone promised fame and fortune. It's how the Camarilla have got most of their dirty jobs done.'

*

Callum fled down the hallway to a bathroom the size of an exhibition hall with busts of the Caesars at each corner. There he lost it, throwing up into a porcelain sink everything he'd eaten since he'd arrived at the villa. He scooped water into his mouth, gulping furiously. Inside the toilet, he lost it again. Everything he'd stomped down inside since Pietra's funeral erupted, racking his body.

34.

NAKED AND NUMB

Andrea knocked on the outside door. '*Signore?*'

Trying to calm himself, Callum rinsed his mouth again before stepping back into the hallway. Signora Orsini led him gently into a smaller salon off the main foyer, where Zach was standing in front of another unlit fireplace. Callum dully noted the same high ceilings and elaborate cornices and borders as the grand foyer. The art on the walls exclusively depicted goddesses: Gabriel Dante Rossetti's Proserpine, Lavinia Fontana's Minerva, Gustave Jean Jacquet's Flora.

'We are under some time pressure here,' said Signora Orsini. 'Tell me where you've hidden the original map and I'll get you safely out of Rome.'

La Madrina seemed genuinely concerned for his well-being. Callum couldn't read Zach, but it didn't matter. He hadn't come this far to run.

'I'm not leaving Rome,' he said. 'I may not be able to find who murdered Pietra, but maybe I can help bring down this Camarilla.' He fixed Signora Orsini with his most insolent look. 'And when I get the rest of the money, you'll get the sketch.'

Zach started forward, but Fiera Orsini cut him off with an angry wave. 'Bring me the map and I'll wire the money immediately.'

Callum stood his ground. He owed Pietra that. 'If you've been watching us, then you know that creating the forgery took all the resources we had. I need the money first.'

Signora Orsini studied him. 'If the Camarilla has a target on your back, it's only a matter of time before they find and kill you too.'

'Then you better keep me alive.'

The sudden fury in *La Madrina*'s expression was terrifying. Callum took a step back.

'You have no idea of the depth into which you've fallen,' she said. 'No idea of the world of hurt you have unleashed on yourself.

'Look around.' She waved her hands at the paintings lining the walls. 'These men and women were once the rock stars and celebrities of the world. They captured the things that mattered, and they helped us understand the world. But we've pushed them to the margins and we are paying the price. Our imaginations have shrivelled and made the world ready for the rise of the Second Kingdom.'

Zach bent his head to his tablet. Before Callum's disbelieving eyes, the naked Minerva in the Fontana painting started to breathe. A shimmering bubble of mist ballooned out from the centre of the canvas, wrapping around Zach and the screen of his tablet.

The goddess stepped out of the painting, dragging her rich brocade robes over her shoulder, a trail of light anchoring her to the canvas. When her feet touched the ground, the light behind her surged back inside the painting. Minerva's flesh filled out and her skin gradually lost its translucence until she was solid and stunning and standing before a gobsmacked Callum, her auburn hair piled in waves on top of her head and held in place with combs of pearls.

Signora Orsini shook her head. 'Really, Zach? It had to be the naked one?'

Zach grinned, set his tablet down, and helped Minerva on with her robes.

Questions were piling up in Callum's mind. 'I need a drink,' he said, rubbing his eyes.

Andrea came into the gallery wheeling a drinks tray, apparently unaffected by Minerva's presence. He offered a glass to Callum, who drank it down in one draft. He was sweating, a combination of shock and fear and whisky burning under his skin, his shirt sticking to his back. A sudden breeze from the open windows made him shiver, and he wiped his forehead with the bottom of his shirt.

Suddenly he hiccupped, finding it difficult to focus. Behind him the gallery door slammed. The shot glass clattered to the floor, and Callum toppled unconscious next to it.

35.

BAD MOON RISING

Luca waited until the moon was low in the night sky before stepping out on to the roof. He raised his hands to the heavens and drank the darkness. Then he soared out over the city and flew west until he spotted the distinctive skyline of Madrid, the four glass and steel towers like standing stones reaching to the heavens.

In darkness, he darted and dipped over the rooftops of the city, only folding his wings as his feet touched down on the roof of the southern entrance of the Museo Nacional del Prado. The statue of Diego Velasquez rocked gently on its foundations. A few couples spread on the grass enjoying the romance of a Spanish night looked up, but they saw only the creep of a shadow before a bank of clouds settled across the moon.

The day long ago when the Inquisitor had lost the lyre, Luca had arrived too late to stop the carnage. He remembered swooping across the Inquisitor's garden, the air ripe with the stench of decay, thousands of beetle shells and carcasses twitching on the black earth. His father's palazzo looked as if a hammer of the gods had flattened the balcony and demolished the entire rear wall. He had come in low and landed on top of the rubble.

'The Moor has the Conjuror,' his father had rasped, shaking with fury. 'And the artist has the lyre. How has this happened? We were so close…' It was only the Inquisitor's malevolence that had kept him alive. 'Get us away from here, Luca. We need to – regroup. I need to heal. *How has this happened*?'

Now the Inquisitor was free again. The scent of oranges and wickedness woven in the warm air inside the Museum of Antiquities still lingered in Luca's senses.

The clouds swirled around Luca as he crouched on the Prado roof. Given what happened to Sebina one hundred years later, he should have left his father to rot with the beetles in that bedroom all those centuries ago.

He placed his palms flat on the roof vents. As soon as he felt a rush of air from below, he tore the heavy steel covers from their hinges.

He pursed his lips and sighed. He hated transforming immediately after flight. Flight was an aphrodisiac firing through ever muscle and organ, quickening his breath. Staring into the darkness below the vent, he wrapped himself in his wings. For a moment too short for the human eye to notice, he was only light. Then, like ice, his wings melted away, leaving Luca naked in his human form.

He dropped feet first into the gallery, landing with a force that sent shock waves throughout the building, knocking plaster gods from their pedestals, iron gates from their stanchions and paintings from the walls. The tremors set the alarms off in the building.

The security lights strobed overhead. The clang of the alarm was deafening. Unconcerned, Luca walked purposefully down the main exhibition hall to the centre of the museum. Night guards began flowing in from the galleries on all sides, but he wordlessly raised his hand, knocking them all out. He removed jackets from two prostrate guards before bending the steel bars that had slammed down in front of the gallery. There wasn't much time. The authorities would be here soon.

Hieronymus Bosch had called it *The Garden of Earthly Delights*. The central panel of the triptych depicted a great phallic fountain rising from an earth-like globe, exotic creatures coupling with faceless humans of all races, lush fruits weighing down the branches of every tree, birds everywhere. It was not symbolism. It was reality. The Eden of the Second Kingdom.

Luca assessed the triptych with a cool eye. He had known about it for centuries, but had never needed to retrieve it until now. Critics had always struggled to make sense of what it meant, but it was simple enough to Luca. On a mission in the south of Spain spying for the Order of Era Mina, Bosch had seen the Inquisitor's garden for himself and painted it from memory: as a warning to the world, and a hiding place for the sacred instrument that the Camarilla needed to open Chaos and raise the other Watchers. The trail for a Conjuror to play the instrument had gone cold for several hundred years, but at last there was another in the world.

Luca would do as he was asked. For now. He was playing a dangerous game with his recent deals and promises. He'd play both sides until the portal was opened, and then he'd strike.

Luca stepped closer to the panel known as 'Musicians' Hell'. He nodded, satisfied by what he saw.

He felt the rush of outside air and heard the wail of sirens as a hundred first responders burst into the building. Luca waved an absent hand at the unconscious guards on the ground. One by one, their heads lolling on their chests, they rose into the air and piled on top of each other, blocking the entrance to the Bosch gallery.

Luca folded the three panels of the altarpiece and wrapped them in the guards' jackets. The nub of his wings stabbed through the flesh beneath his shoulder blades. With his arms around the triptych, he shot through the open vent in the roof overhead with two silent beats of his great silver-black wings.

LONDON

SATURDAY

36.

FLOWER OF SCOTLAND

In her pink coat, matching pillbox hat with a spray of heather on its brim, a boxy handbag hooked over her forearm, and her gloved hands crossed in front of her, an elderly woman headed down a set of private stairs at the Royal Academy of Arts in London to interrupt a meeting.

Minutes earlier, she had faded from a Degas painting hung in a private gallery on the top floor of the RA building, a room few knew existed and even fewer knew held an enchanted work of art through which an old woman could travel. She brushed paint flakes from her coat, repositioned her hat, and walked smartly towards the guards flanking the doors of the Council Chamber. Her determination trailed behind her in ribbons of blue light. Even in her seventies, Jeannie Butler remained one of the most powerful women in the world, her supernatural abilities unprecedented but rarely seen.

The guards stepped in front of the doors, blocking her passage.

'I'm sorry, Ma'am,' said the younger guard stolidly. 'But we have orders that under no circumstances are the Assembly proceedings to be interrupted, especially at this critical stage.'

'Critical indeed,' Jeannie Butler snorted. 'The fate of the Calder siblings, maybe even of our kind is on the table here. Move aside now.'

She took a stride closer.

The older of the two guards stuttered, 'But Ma'am, the Council has already begun its deliberations. Sir Giles has made it quite clear we mustn't allow anyone to enter. Not even you.'

'Ach, fer goodness sake,' said Jeannie, her Scottish accent ramping up her already intimidating presence. 'Yer really going tae do this, Bill? It is Bill, am I right?'

She was at least half the older guard's size and weight, but she appeared to tower over him. He nodded, nervously.

'Well, Bill,' Jeannie went on. 'Ye ken I must get inside that room.' She slipped off one of her gloves, resting her bare hand on his forearm. 'I can insist ye open this door, but if I do you'll feel disoriented, sick, and awfie dizzy for a good couple of hours. Maybe you'll even black out for a wee while. I'd rather not inspirit ye in that way.'

Bill pursed his lips and sighed audibly. 'You'll need to surrender your phone and any drawing materials.'

'My purse has only a wee bit money and a lipstick in it.'

133

Jeannie unclicked her bag and held it open. Bill nodded to the other guard. Together, they pulled open the double doors.

Inside the room, seven members of the European Council of Guardians sat on high-backed chairs around a carved medieval table set for twelve. All heads turned. Sir Giles Grafton the Council director, jumped to his feet. But before he could get any words out, the two guards slammed the doors closed and relocked them.

'This is an outrageous violation of protocol, Jeannie,' Sir Giles said, his neck mottling red. 'We are still hearing Vaughn's testimony.'

Jeannie noted the Guardians at the table were dressed in their ceremonial velvet robes, each one with an ancient silver and a gold coin placed in front of them. She nodded at the handsome forty-year-old man at the far end of the table, shaggy dark hair combed off his face. Vaughn Grant, director of Orion, had a style that usually leaned towards biker-chic. Today, he looked uptight in a black bespoke suit and blue shirt open at the neck, his hands flat on the table. His adrenaline hummed in her head like a small generator.

'Besides, you're too late,' Sir Giles added. A pewter vessel the size of a tea caddy etched with the symbol of a flying stag on its lid was gripped in his hands. 'We were about to dismiss Mr Grant from the table.'

'But ye haven't voted yet.' Jeannie indicated the gold and silver coins on the table. When an Animare broke Council rules, the coins were placed inside the pewter vessel: gold for guilty, silver for not. 'So my timing is impeccable.'

She removed her other glove, making deliberate eye contact with each of the men and women seated at the table. Apart from the Italian representative, Luigi Silvestri, a distinguished art historian and the Council's second-in-command, they all looked to their laps instead of meeting her penetrating stare.

The walls of the Council Chamber were draped in richly embroidered tapestries, each telling the history of the Order of Era Mina. Jeannie walked the length of the room, stretching out her hand as she moved. When her fingers touched the tapestries, threads began to twinkle and robed figures shimmied until one by one, kings, queens, warriors, and knights danced to life. Mythical beasts, big and small, with horns and without, breathing fire inside mountains or swimming deep under oceans whose names had long been forgotten, twitched and tugged against the dark embroidered cloth like constellations against the night sky.

Jeannie abhorred the Council's binding ritual. Trapping an Animare inside a painting forever for breaking Council rules was medieval and monstrous, benefitting no one except those in power. She surmised that she wasn't alone in thinking this, to judge from the half-empty room. The Council's power was slipping.

'Jeannie,' said Sir Giles, moderating his tone a little. 'You can't stop this vote.'

Jeannie caught a subtle nod from Vaughn as he looked up from his smart watch.

'Ah'm no here to instigate a coup,' she said. 'Ah'm hear to save our lives.'

Sir Giles snorted. 'Don't be so bloody dramatic.'

At the final tapestry Jeannie paused, letting her fingers linger on the stitching of a female warrior perched on the highest rampart of a castle keep. She deliberately traced the warrior's bow and arrow as it lifted to shoot a demonic rider on a flying black stag with eyes like hot coals and orange flames streaming from its hooves. The girl's head turned and an embroidered eye winked.

Sir Giles slammed his hands on the table. 'Enough! This display in front of the men and women about to pass judgement on the future of Orion and its agents is diabolical. Those two *delinquents* left an unforgivable mess at the Castel Sant'Angelo in Rome. They cannot be allowed to run wild any longer.'

His rage hit Jeannie in a current of charged air, knocking her hat from her head.

'*Diabolical*?' she echoed. 'It seems tae me, given the threat we're facing, that you should not be using that word so lightly.

'You know that in recent months, musical instruments have been disappearing from paintings all over the world? The Camarilla is searching for the lyre. These thefts, together with the failed attempt in Italy to bind the Conjuror, should be more than enough evidence for you to act *with* Orion, not *against* us.' Jeannie lowered her voice to a furious whisper. '*With* us, Giles. Do you understand?'

Ripples of static crackled over the tapestries. The frisson of electricity stretched over the centre of the table between Sir Giles and Jeannie.

'There have always been rogue Animare loose and working for their own gain,' blustered Sir Giles. 'You know that as well as I do. That they are part of a secret army called the Camarilla. Ridiculous.'

Jeannie picked up her hat, sprucing the heather on its band with her fingers, her anger rising. Vaughn shifted forward in his seat, his hands in his lap.

'Sit down, Giles,' she said with an irritated sigh.

She took the empty chair next to Silvestri. Sir Giles remained standing. Jeannie unbuttoned her coat and set her hat and gloves on her lap. All around the room, the figures on the tapestries turned to watch.

'Yer missing a few Council members, I see,' Jeannie remarked. 'Have they seen this assembly for what it is? A cover-up?'

Sir Giles breathed heavily. 'The rest of the Council is otherwise occupied.'

'Don't lie tae me. You've lost their support for this reckless retribution. Or worse, you've lost their allegiance altogether and they're siding with our enemies.'

'This Council has the right to protect our kind from those who would do us harm!' Sir Giles spluttered.

'As far as I'm concerned, Orion has become a cabal of unregulated power, not the Camarilla.'

Jeannie gave a humourless laugh. 'That's as absurd a statement as it is a dangerous one! The Camarilla are gathering their forces on our horizon, Giles. There will be chaos if we don't work together.'

Sir Giles banged the pewter container on the table, its vibrations scattering nearby coins. 'We've already heard Vaughn's testimony in defence of Orion,' he said, his lip curling. 'These stories of a Second Kingdom on earth, the enslavement of humanity – it's preposterous! The Camarilla was neutralized during the Inquisition and, Vaughn assures me, crushed again more recently in Spain. A crushing, let me remind you, for which Orion agents were the only witnesses!'

'What of events at the Castel Sant'Angelo in Rome last month?' inquired a soft German voice.

Jeannie noticed Vaughn flinch as Sir Giles turned to Kristopher Gilligan.

'A proven radical terror attack,' Gilligan said firmly. 'Nothing to do with the Camarilla.'

'Orion is attempting to distract us from the seriousness of the twins' continued irresponsibility,' added Silvestri, fussing with his bow tie. 'And as for that poor young man from America, are we really to believe that he is a... a *Conjuror*?'

Jeannie felt Vaughn's rage slam into her Spanish neighbour, who rocked back a little in his chair.

The Council's newest member, Professor Ernestina Vershelden from Amsterdam, clasped her hands together on the table. The gold bracelets adorning her wrists chimed against each other like bells. 'With all due respect, Mrs Butler,' she said in her lightly accented English, 'Mr Grant's testimony about fallen angels manipulating Animare and Guardians to resurrect a second paradise on earth are myths for our art and stories. Nothing more. We should vote on the matter at hand.'

Jeannie picked up Professor Vershelden's gold coin and rolled it over her fingers, like a street magician. The image of the peryton etched on one side alternated with a spiral on the other. Then she set the coin down.

'You'll listen to me willingly,' she said. 'Besides it'll take me too long to inspirit all of ye, and time is'nae on our side.' She snapped open her handbag and withdrew a series of photographs from beneath the lining which she slid down the table to Sir Giles.

The Council Director grabbed them and looked. His face contorted. The mist hovering above the table crackled with bolts of angry light but began to fizzle the longer Sir Giles stared at the photos. Professor Vershelden extracted the first photograph from Sir Giles' hand, holding it as if it was contagious.

'That is a Nephilim,' Jeannie said. 'Half-angel, half-human. He took human form in order to steal Hieronymus Bosch's *Garden of Earthly Delights* from the Prado last night.'

Sir Giles' face was white. 'Nephilim?' he repeated.

'Look it up, you daft bugger,' snapped Jeannie. 'I take it Mr Grant here included the pertinent fact that Orpheus's lyre – the lyre required by the Camarilla to open Chaos and bring about the Second Kingdom – was hidden inside the third panel of this painting?'

The expressions around the table confirmed it. As the shocked murmurs began to spread, Jeannie noticed Vaughn slipping his phone into his pocket. He gave her an imperceptible nod.

'Quiet!' Jeannie cried, her hands in the air as she waved for calm. The threads on all the tapestries lit up like a million strands of lights – flashing, warning. 'You have to listen to me now, before hell breaks loose.'

37.

TIME'S NOT ON OUR SIDE

Thirty minutes later, Vaughn Grant stood outside the gates of the Royal Academy courtyard, catching his breath before threading through the heavy morning traffic on Piccadilly. Ducking inside the tea shop on the corner of Duke Street, he smiled to the young woman behind the counter.

'Usual, love?' she asked.

'Please,' said Vaughn, before taking the table in the bay window where the chairs were decorative wrought iron and extremely uncomfortable. Anyone taller than six feet had to sit back a few metres to avoid their knees bumping the iron swirls on the matching table. For Vaughn, the ambiance was part of the place's charm. That, and the fact that the same family had run the establishment since the eighteenth century and tended to ignore the occasional supernatural occurrence across the street.

Only one other table was occupied with three elderly women, enjoying the last sitting for afternoon tea, Harrods shopping bags in a green row beneath their table. Dunking his chocolate biscuits in his coffee, Vaughn thought about what just happened across the street. If it hadn't been for Jeannie's presence, Vaughn was not sure things would have gone Orion's way. And they had to go Orion's way. Recent events had proved that.

The door to the tea shop chimed and a young woman in a navy linen suit, skinny trousers cuffed over black combat boots and a tapered jacket over a silk T-shirt came in, scanning the room from behind dark sunglasses before heading to Vaughn's table.

Lakshmi Misra unbuttoned her jacket and took the seat across from Vaughn. A radio was hooked to the belt of her trousers and her boots were polished to a mirrored shine. In her late twenties, Lakshmi was one of Scotland Yard's youngest Inspectors in the Art and Antiquities unit. More importantly, she was one of a small trusted group of people in positions of power in the UK who were privy to Orion's secrets. These positions and their covert responsibilities were hereditary to families known as Patrons of Era Mina.

She silenced her radio. 'You were right,' she said, leaning towards Vaughn. 'Your Nephilim, Luca Ferrante, was responsible for the recent theft at the Prado.'

'How much time before the press know about it?'

'The Prado's not keen on the publicity, so we should have enough time. How much do you need?'

'As much as I can get,' said Vaughn, grimly. 'If Luca took the lyre on the Camarilla's behalf, then time isn't on our side.' He roughed his fingers through his hair. 'Dammit! We should have taken the triptych ourselves the moment we identified Bosch from Matt's sketch. Now we're playing catch-up. Again.'

'Not completely,' said Lakshmi. 'If this plan works, we may just get ahead of the curve.'

Vaughn ordered two more coffees and an Eccles cake, Lakshmi's favourite. 'Do we have time to eat?' she asked, raising slim eyebrows.

'If you're quick.'

The waiter set down the fresh coffee and pastries. Orion's failure to act sooner on their intel weighed heavily on Vaughn. It was why he was here with Lakshmi, and why he'd persuaded Jeannie to leave the Abbey and come to London. If they were going to stop the Camarilla, Orion had to act boldly. Orion had to take more risks. Orion needed to finish what they had started the day Rémy Dupree Rush arrived in London. He rolled his neck, loosening his knotted muscles.

'When was the last time you had more than a couple of hours of sleep?' Lakshmi asked.

'I'll sleep when this is over. The Camarilla's offensive has started. With the lyre and the Inquisitor's portrait already in Rome, all they need is Rémy and they can open Chaos.'

Three Panda cars shot past the window heading west, their sirens wailing and lights flashing. Within seconds three more and an ambulance screamed past in the other direction. The traffic was clogged and moving slowly. Vaughn turned back to Lakshmi, her radio crackling with angry voices.

'The Camarilla still need the Devil's Interval, the sacred chord for Rémy to play on the lyre,' Lakshmi pointed out.

Vaughn relaxed a little. 'At least we have that locked away.'

'And Rémy? He's locked away too?'

'In a Glasgow safe-house under Alessandro's surveillance.'

'Have you told them about your plan?'

'Not yet.'

'They'll be pissed off.'

'I'll take that risk. By the way,' he added as he lifted his cup, 'excellent work in Rome last month.'

Lakshmi tilted her head, acknowledging his praise.

'In fact,' Vaughn added, 'your team was so thorough that the Council itself bought the terrorist theory. It caused a bit of a problem.'

'Oops,' Lakshmi said, stirring sugar into her cup. She finished her cake, wiping crumbs from her lap. Her radio squawked. She turned down the volume. 'Orion has someone inside the Camarilla, right?'

'We do,' said Vaughn, dropping money on to the table.

'Then you'll know their next move as soon as they're ready to make it.'

'Provided they don't catch our someone first,' said Vaughn.

A red double-decker bus trundled to a stop near the RA. Then a tactical vehicle wailed past the tea-shop window, jumped the curb and swerved on to the pavement. Its passengers, in full SWAT gear, leapt from the vehicle before it came to a halt, waving furiously at the bus driver to move. Two London taxis and a delivery truck passed the other way, heading for Piccadilly Circus.

'No turning back now,' said Lakshmi. 'Everything's in place.'

A halo of energy was hovering above the RA buildings. It expanded like a balloon, then exploded, engulfing the buildings and the grounds with tentacles of light and colour.

38.

BLOW OUT

Every building, vehicle and ribbon of pavement wavered, as if someone had lifted the corner of the Royal Academy courtyard like the edge of a tablecloth and shaken away the crumbs. The only sounds within the blast radius were the muffled screams of pedestrians and the dulled squeal of skidding cars. Where there should have been sound there was only colour: layers of brilliant blue and gold, shimmering silver and glowing neon. Silent ripples of light radiated into the street, narrowly missing the double-decker bus as it flipped over and over until it came to a halt right side up on top of a line of empty parked cars. The glass in the tea-shop window sighed and slid out of its frame, smashing on the pavement outside.

Vaughn did what he could to calm the elderly tea drinkers. 'Can you handle the fallout, Lakshmi?' he asked, making for the tea-shop door.

Lakshmi was already seeing to the waiter, who was

stunned but unhurt. 'Of course,' she said over her shoulder. 'Go!'

The upended double-decker was empty. It looked as if it had been on its way to pick up a tour group. The lone driver was crawling out of his smashed front window. The staff from the nearby hotel were outside in full force, swarming into the street to offer aid to the people in the multiple but minor car collisions. Vaughn climbed over the rubble of the collapsed archway into the Royal Academy courtyard and surveyed the damage.

The whole area was covered in glass from blown-out windows. Two of the courtyard sculptures had projectiles embedded in them. A big black hole had been punched in the ground, an abyss with silver spider veins flowing from its edges deep into the darkness. Every building in the main square was relatively unscathed, windows notwithstanding, with the exception of the one that had stood immediately above the hole.

The Council Chamber.

The hole looked like it was breathing. Like it was alive.

The Academy staff were already moving inside in recovery mode. Emergency lights had kicked on and first responders' whistles were piercing the eerie quiet. Vaughn darted across the courtyard, drawing as he ran. When he got to the tallest building in the compound, a fire-escape animated against its rear wall. He shoved his sketchpad back in his pocket and climbed the ladder two at a time. Then he flattened himself on the roof and army-crawled to the edge.

Vaughn's fingers flashed across his sketchpad, and a military pair of binoculars manifested in front of him in a burst of light. Putting them to his eyes, he watched Lakshmi cordon off the area, barking orders at the police and fire officers who'd arrived on the scene with her cell phone caught between her ear and her shoulder. This was why Orion paid handsomely to have friends in high places.

Vaughn watched the strange cloud formation coiling over the nearby buildings. Then, like the trails of a jet, the clouds thinned out across the northern sky.

SCOTLAND

39.

LIFE'S PLEASURES

Caravaggio pulled himself up against the hundred pillows piled against Matt's headboard. He yanked one from under his shoulders, balled it up and tossed it onto the floor in disgust. 'What is it with this century and pillows?'

Matt handed Caravaggio a beer. 'Stop complaining. You're lucky to still be in this century.' Pulling on his jeans, he lifted his own beer from the night stand and walked to the open window to look out over the Scottish hillside.

'I may be lucky,' said the artist with a smirk. 'But so are you, my friend.'

Matt ignored this. 'We need to leave Orion HQ and head back to Glasgow tomorrow, before Vaughn realizes we all took a little holiday.'

'Why would you ever want to go back?'

Caravaggio climbed out of bed, stepping over the clothing strewn on the floor. He lifted Matt's chin. Matt met his gaze, his irises fragmenting into a kaleidoscope of electric blues.

'Why not just come away with me?' Caravaggio suggested, kissing Matt on the lips. 'We could wander the world.' He moved his lips to Matt's neck. 'Enjoy life's pleasures.'

Matt leaned into the kiss, then gently pushed the artist away. 'Because Michele, I don't trust you.'

The artist pouted and helped himself to a slug of Matt's beer.

'I like you,' Matt amended. 'I like you a lot. But you're dangerous to be around.'

He pulled on a vintage Dylan tour T-shirt of his dad's. The dates were faded and unreadable, but Matt refused to get rid of it. Em thought he wore the shirts as penance for their father's death. Matt was holding on to the idea that it was all about the aesthetic.

The sun bathed the tiny oval room in a pale pink light. Matt slipped on his shades. 'Let's go for a walk,' he suggested.

Caravaggio sighed. 'If you don't want to pick up where I just left off, fresh air will have to suffice... for now. Let me get dressed.'

Matt was already halfway down the narrow spiral stairs when the tower shook on its foundations, throwing him down the stone steps. His head thumped against the wall at the bottom. Before he blacked out, he heard the whir of a great pair of wings.

40.

OUT COLD

Matt could smell the sea, feel his body rising and falling in angry waves. He was at the helm of a sailboat, its jib full and holding taut against a strong wind, Era Mina in the distance, the light on top of the tower flashing directly into his eyes. Then it wasn't Era Mina any more. It was the church tower at Orion headquarters. And he wasn't on a sailboat. He was on the ground and Caravaggio was dousing him with cold water.

Matt sputtered and coughed, rolling on to his back and gazing up at the late afternoon sky. They were a short distance from what was left of the tower, and the sun striped through the trees above his head. He felt dizzy and nauseated. He covered his eyes and tried to sit up. Caravaggio handed him his shades. Matt put them gratefully on his nose.

'What the hell happened?'

'Bad things,' said Caravaggio grimly. 'And more may be coming.'

Matt tried standing, but his legs wouldn't cooperate. He crawled against an oak tree. Over Caravaggio's shoulder, Orion HQ was burning. Strange white flames like long pale fingers were pulling the structure into a hole as big as a football pitch that was widening beneath it. The church tower itself had gone, a black scar on the ground the only evidence it ever existed.

'That's not a normal fire,' mumbled Matt, touching the egg-sized lump at the back of his head.

'No. It is not,' agreed Caravaggio. 'That's a supernatural inferno.' The artist was fully dressed, his leather jacket fastened over his loose white tunic and leather trousers.

'How long was I unconscious?'

'A few minutes.' He handed Matt a scuffed black sketchpad and tapped the dagger in his waistband. 'I managed to save a couple of things.'

Matt watched groggily as the black scar on the courtyard between the buildings healed over and vanished. He ran his fingers over the imprint of the constellation of Orion on the sketchpad cover. 'Thanks,' he said after a moment. 'For getting me out.'

Caravaggio pulled Matt to his feet and helped him through the woods and away from the imploded church.

'Where are we going?' said Matt, feeling light-headed and bruised all over.

'Far away.' Caravaggio led Matt through the trees. 'A vanishing church is going to bring attention up here very soon. I don't think we want to be explaining what may or may not have happened.'

Matt grimaced. 'Yeah,' he said. 'Especially since we're still supposed to be in Glasgow.'

He realized they were both barefoot. Waiting until they were out of sight of the emergency vehicles squealing through the village and up the winding one-lane road towards the church, Matt opened his sketchpad to a blank page where he drew a pair of black CAT work boots for him and a pair of riding boots for Caravaggio.

'You didn't happen to rescue my phone, did you?' asked Matt.

'Never crossed my mind,' said Caravaggio, admiring his shimmering boots.

''Course it didn't.'

The higher and deeper they tramped into the forest, the darker it became and the less nauseous Matt felt. But as they climbed, he felt the atmosphere change. The air grew heavier, denser, warmer. The stench of sulphur was stronger. It reminded Matt of something from a long time ago. He spun on his heels.

'I feel it too,' said Caravaggio quietly.

Matt nodded, relieved. It wasn't just him.

Leaves crunched and the ground shook somewhere on the hill behind them. Bursts of smoke coughed through the trees. Then the trees didn't just rustle; they bowed over, their tops brushing the ground before whipping back up.

Saying nothing, Matt and Caravaggio split up, ducked into the brush and hid behind the trees. Matt signalled with a headshake and a scribble not to animate; the animation glow would give away their hiding places— *Shit*. Animating the boots had been a beacon to whoever was tracking them.

Matt scanned the thick growth off the trail. Further up the slope, he noticed a stone bothy used by hikers and hunters. If they could get inside, the glow from their animated boots would no longer be visible. But to get to the bothy would mean climbing higher directly in front of whatever was hunting them. Which was a problem.

Unless…

41.

SYNC AND SWIM

On the other side of Scotland, Rémy pulled his earbuds out while dragging a kayak one-handed on to the sand. He peered into the dark mouth of the cave on the western shore of Auchinmurn.

'So this is where the magic happened,' he said.

He and Em had taken the train from Glasgow to Largs early, enjoying the hour of relative normality in the quiet train car, chatting a little about their childhoods, listening to music on their phones and reading. The Abbey had been deserted with Jeannie in London for the Council meeting and Renard visiting a friend in America, so they'd spent most of the day raking through stacks of ancient manuscripts and mounds of scrolls in search of clues to the prophecy on the stone relief in Rome. To Rémy's disappointment, they had found nothing to illuminate the bits and pieces he'd already uncovered in his mother's journal. The sun streaming into the windows from the bay and the smell of summer in the warm breeze proved too much for either of them to sit inside and dig through the last stack of manuscripts, and so they had decided to get out on the water instead, Rémy kayaking while Em swam.

'Yup,' said Em, dropping her swim goggles to her neck. 'This is the place. The cave where the infamous Calder twins at the ripe age of thirteen ran a long con on tourists to the island of Auchinmurn.'

'How much money did you make?' Rémy sat on a flat rock just inside the lip of the cave and dangled his feet into one of the many pools pocking the rocky ground.

'About two hundred quid,' said Em, offering Rémy a square of the energy bar she was unwrapping. He shook his head.

'I'd rather eat sand.'

'Yeah,' she held up the energy bar, 'but raisins.'

He shivered. 'Not happening. Hate them.'

'Who doesn't like raisins?'

'It's a black thing.'

'Really?' she said, sheepishly.

'Of course not.'

Rémy's laughter made Em grin. He felt warm. He was glad the four of them had been at each other's throats in Glasgow yesterday. It made it easier to spend time alone with Em. Maybe today he could say some of the things he hadn't brought up in the garden back in Glasgow. Because no matter what they found in the Abbey's manuscripts, Rémy was determined to go back to Rome.

'So what the hell's wrong with raisins?' Em prompted.

157

'When I was in kindergarten,' Rémy explained, 'I used to save the box of raisins my aunt packed in my lunch and hide them in my desk for later. Sometimes I'd forget they were there. I was sneaking some during Geography when suddenly the kid next to me fainted. Turns out my desk was full of ants and I was eating them. Ants were all up in my neck and arms.'

Em looked twice at her energy bar, shrugged, then popped the rest in her mouth.

Rémy tilted the brim of his Chicago Bulls cap and wiped the sweat from his forehead. 'Conning tourists is a dope way to make money,' he said. 'By the time I figured out what I could do with my voice and music, a demon was chasing me across the world.'

'Mum made us donate the money to the primary school in Largs.'

'And your friend, Zach,' said Rémy, bringing Em's ex-boyfriend carefully into the conversation. 'He helped with the con?'

'Couldn't have done it without him.' Em's voice was surprisingly steady, Rémy thought, given that Zach had almost got them killed in Rome. 'He created the sound effects and the 3D images that made the tourists think the pictures in the performance were all digital when, in fact, Matt and I were animating. We thought we were so clever.'

'Pretty ingenious.'

'Until a kid got hurt. Then no more nice things.' Em picked a grey stone, walked to the mouth of the cave and skimmed the rock out across the bay. It skipped once, twice, three times across the water. She turned, giving a sad and broken smile. 'I know you're convinced it was Zach and his mum in that tomb with you, but I can't see it. He was always one of us.'

'Until he wasn't.'

Sitting this close to Em, Rémy could see the freckles dusting the bridge of her nose and the way her cheeks stood out against her pale white skin. Goggle indentations rimmed her striking emerald eyes like targets. Her short hair was wet and sticking out in every direction. She was beautiful. Not in the classic, breathtaking way his mom had been, but in the way he realized he was more and more attracted to. He buried the desire as soon as it surfaced and tried to think instead about how well-adjusted she was to her supernatural powers, even more confident in her abilities than her brother. For all his physical bravado, Matt was much more insecure.

Early education was the key, Rémy decided. They'd had time and training behind them. Rémy still felt a bit like the man who fell to earth with no clue about the world he'd fallen into.

He thought about leaning closer and kissing Em, but crushed the thought, letting a few bars of a Julian Vaughn melody curl across his consciousness. There was Zach to consider. Em claimed she was no longer in love with him, which Rémy believed. Kind of. But that was only a small part of the issue. Was Zach hunting them or helping them? No one seemed to know.

Em frowned at him, finger-combing her wet hair from her forehead. 'What?'

Rémy was afraid she'd snagged the tail of his desire with her keen empathic abilities. 'Nothing... just thinking.' *Idiot. That was your chance.*

Em was still gazing at him. Rémy cast around for something to say.

'So the Council meeting,' he blurted. 'In London. The one Jeannie and Vaughn are at. Do you really think they'll vote to shut down Orion because of what I did in Rome? What happened was my fault.'

Em shrugged. 'We're running around without Guardians to keep us in check like most other Animare. The Council hates that. So probably, yes. Doesn't mean we'll let them though.' She grinned. 'Anyway, Jeannie says there are more important things the Council should be worrying about.'

'Like the coming of the Second Kingdom and the end of the world as we know it?'

Em laughed. 'Something like that.'

The wind was picking up, the warm sun flitting in and out of light white clouds, but beyond the tower on the smaller island of Era Mina, a storm was brooding on the horizon. A rogue wave slapped against Rémy's beached kayak.

Em tucked the energy-bar wrapper into the waterproof pouch belted at her waist. 'We should get back to the

Abbey before it storms,' she said, settling the swim goggles back on her face.

Rémy dragged his kayak into the shallow water, adjusted his life-jacket and eased his long legs inside. He was tall and fit in the way he imagined his dad had been. He'd never known his dad, but he'd heard stories about his athleticism and competitive streak: traits Rémy had inherited. Everything else came from his mother: his brown Creole skin, and his terrible fear that he'd fall into the madness that had consumed her if he didn't bring this to an end.

Em dived under, coming up for air metres into the bay. Rémy manoeuvred the kayak around to her right, keeping a barrier between her and the open sea. She was taking a breath every four strokes, and Rémy timed his paddling accordingly. They were in sync as they approached the Abbey's dock.

Rémy suddenly heard a squeal like an injured animal. It pierced his earbud, and he dropped his paddle. Em's head shot out of the water.

'Did you hear that?' said Rémy.

Em's eyes were wide. 'I felt it under the water. What—'

A massive ball of white light dropped out of the storm cloud and hit the Abbey tower. It sent a shock wave in a kind of slow motion out across the lawn, rippling the grass in waves, coming towards the dock, imploding everything in its wake.

'Em!' screamed Rémy. 'Get out of the water!'

42.

THE DOCK OF THE BAY

Rémy yanked the belt at Em's waist. Seconds before the concussion from the explosion hit the dock, popping up each plank one after the other, he raised her out of the water and – with every muscle screaming – held her as a wave of electricity rocked the kayak.

'Don't move or we'll capsize.'

He kept his balance. Em held herself motionless. When the dangerous ripples of energy had sucked all the water from the shoreline, leaving jelly fish popped on the hard sand like used balloons, Rémy dropped Em on to the sand.

'Run!' he shouted.

They both sprinted for the shore. Behind them, the water gathered itself into a giant tsunami and began to chase them down like a thundering freight train. They scrambled on to the Abbey lawn and kept running. The wave hit them midway up the lawn and pulled them into its surging current, dragging them violently back out into the bay.

Rémy and Em fought the current and eventually dragged themselves back up on to the soaking lawn. The wooden jetty was floating in pieces. One of the walls of the boat shed had been blown out. The Abbey speedboat was undamaged, but off its moorings and halfway across the bay.

Em sprinted towards the rubble of the tower. By the time Rémy caught up, she was bent over, vomiting into what was left of the rose garden. Gently, he rubbed her back, staring into the black pulsing hole where the west tower had stood. Loose papers fluttered like doves out of the abyss.

'Oh God,' Em croaked. 'My grandfather's study... And the vault. The vault was below the tower. All that priceless art entrusted to our care, all those manuscripts...'

The rim of the hole was shifting and sliding into the abyss.

'It's closing in on itself,' Rémy warned.

'We need to save the art!'

Her rage shrieked like a banshee inside Rémy's head. 'I don't think there's anything we can do,' he said.

Rocks and rubble and even the nearby rose plants were getting sucked down into the darkness. Rémy tried to pull her away from the precipice. But Em jerked her arm away, lost her footing and slipped over the side. Her hands scrabbled for a stone, a root, anything to stop falling further into the blackness. Rémy lunged at her arms and missed. His head was a cacophony, like notes shredding on a guitar.

'Rémy!'

The hole was contracting. Em still wasn't getting any traction. Closing his eyes, Rémy pulled out his harmonica and played. The music amplified in a pulsing haze that quickly surrounded the hole. A rope appeared at his feet. Knotting it quickly around his waist, he dug his feet into what was left of the garden path and tossed the end into the thickening mist.

'Take the end, Em!' he bellowed. 'Em! Em?'

43.

WONDERWALL

Em grasped the rope and Rémy yanked her back to safe ground as the hole closed with a faint sizzle of light. Not even the foundation wall of the tower was left standing. It was as if the ground had swallowed it whole. Without its tower, the Abbey looked as if the structure had lost a limb.

Rémy wiped his bloody nose in the evaporating mist. Recovery from a conjuring often involved a nosebleed. It was generally a price worth paying. He'd read in his mom's diary how conjuring depleted her energy so much she'd sometimes sleep for fifteen hours straight.

A high wall with ivy weaving in and out of the bricks surrounded what was left of the Abbey compound, stretching from the main road to the water, enclosing the woods and the rocky beach. The ivy was ablaze in light, each leaf radiating like green bulbs on a Christmas tree. Strange-looking storm clouds stretched over the islands in the bay, shading the summer sky a peculiar turquoise blue.

Em wiped her grimy arm across her teary eyes. 'Whoever did this is still nearby.'

'I know,' said Rémy. 'Look at that sky.'

'It's not just the sky.' Dirt and small rocks were embedded in her skin. 'The ivy on the walls is an animation. It reacts to strangers and supernatural beings. Zach designed it. It's a kind of digital-organic hybrid invention of his.'

Rémy took Em's hand. They walked towards the kitchens, carefully scouting the area for movement. As they reached the middle of the lawn, the ground began to move under their feet. The lawn rippled at first, then it tore itself up from the shoreline as if an invisible hand was rolling up a rug.

As they pelted towards the French doors into the kitchen, fingers of light crawled out of the scar in the ground left by the tower, sending white flames snaking through the entire top floor of the Abbey. The peryton flag on the roof snapped defiantly in the wind.

'Our bedrooms,' gasped Em. 'They're on fire.'

She was still in her swimsuit. No paper. No pen. Rémy was in basketball shorts with only his harmonica in his pocket. The ivy on the wall was blazing, twitching. Fingers of fire curled over the roof of the Abbey, the sky like neon above them, the strange storm clouds close enough to touch.

'I need something sharp,' said Em, running towards the ivy-covered wall.

Rémy was soaked with sweat and fear, humming just to keep calm. He whistled a jazz riff and a small box cutter fell from the music to the ground. Em grabbed it. The heat from above was intense, the fingers of flames crawling closer.

At the base of the wall, Em sliced through the skin on the pad under her left thumb, letting her blood fill her palm. Then she closed her eyes and shoved her bloody hand deep into the soil.

'Come on,' she muttered. 'Come on. I need you.'

The strange clouds exploded in blinding colours. A great white peryton swooped out of the rainbow vortex, its antlers wide and branching. And right behind the flying stag, the Nephilim took shape in the bruised, fractured sky.

Luca Ferrante's wingspan was as wide as the compound. A fiery ash cloud stretched and swirled like strips of blood-splattered bandages around him. His face was human but not, his skin stretched across his skull, his hair pure blinding light. The peryton bucked beneath him, its white rack of antlers flaring with light. Powerful as it was, it was no match for the Nephilim.

'Oh, God!' Em pulled her hand from the soil and covered her mouth. 'He'll kill it.'

Not knowing what else to do, Rémy began to sing. His voice lifted from a place deep inside, rising out of him in waves of chilling blue mist. His notes engulfed the peryton. Its wing span broadened. By the time Rémy had hit high C, causing the compound wall itself to shake and crumble, the peryton was as large as the Nephilim.

It tossed its antlers and charged.

The sky screeched. The wall collapsed almost in slow motion, sending clouds of green dust into the air. Em fell to the ground, covering her ears, her face contorted in pain. Rémy heard the terrible sound, but it was somehow muted in his own head. He gave Em his battered iPod and earbuds, cranking the music as loud as she could stand. Then he grabbed her hand and pulled her away from the crumbling wall and out to the centre of the lawn. Visibility was almost nil. The clouds were alive with fire, hanging close to the ground, raining hot ash. It looked as if a volcano was erupting in the atmosphere.

'The peryton!' Em shouted, staring up into the terrible whirling clouds. 'Rémy, what's happening?'

Rémy wiped hot ash from his face. 'We need to get out from under this dangerous sky.'

'We can't leave it,' said Em stubbornly.

'We have to.'

Rémy dragged Em towards the row of art studios running along the cloisters of the Abbey. He grabbed a rock and smashed open the padlock of the first one he came to, shoving Em inside ahead of him.

The studio hadn't been used in a while and was empty, except for a stack of white stretched canvases leaning against one wall and boxes of paint supplies stacked near an easel. The stone floor was filthy and the walls were bare.

'Your hand's still bleeding,' said Rémy as Em sat on a box and bowed her head.

'I'll be fine.' She wiped her palm on the front of her swimsuit and shivered. 'But clothes would be great.'

Rémy wrapped his arms around her before singing a soft bluesy Nina Simone melody, a song his mom had always sung to him when he needed comforting.

'My baby just cares for me...'

A veil of fog uncoiled slowly at Rémy's feet, misty ribbons of yellows, reds, blues and white threading into shapes on the stone. When his voice faded, jeans, T-shirts and two pair of boots sat in a neat pile on the floor, plus a green cardigan with big pockets for Em. They dressed quickly in separate shadowy corners.

'Matches your eyes,' Rémy remarked, handing her the cardigan.

'It's too big,' said Em. She smiled and wrapped it around her body. 'Just the way I like it.'

The door flew open suddenly, in a wind gust so powerful it blew out the window behind them, showering the ground with shards of glass. All the vines of ivy that remained on the external walls stood upright like arrowheads, pointing to the sky.

44.

SMOKE ON THE WATER

The sweet heavenly voice that had come from the ground. Luca whirled about. The Conjuror was here? He could take him...

Before he could fully process the thought into action, the peryton stabbed her antlers deep into Luca's side. He howled, filling the sky with his agony, twisting and swooping as he tried to escape. He couldn't. They were locked together. With the sky a deep purple behind him, Luca made a full transformation to his bestial self. His massive torso stretched and scaled over, the silver edges of his black wings hardened to diamond stilettos and his long-tapered hands became claws. His hair flamed behind him, setting the clouds on fire, his fury raging through the atmosphere. *These islands were meant to be deserted.*

He grasped the jagged antlers in order to wrangle the beast, but they were colder than ice and held a charge that shot up his torso, lighting up his scales. For an instant, he lost feeling in his tapered fingers. He tore his claws away. The peryton's eyes were hard as glass, glazed as if fired in some great kiln. The beast was focused with a power Luca hadn't faced in a long time. Numbness began to creep through his body. She was freezing him from the inside out. He somersaulted desperately through the deep purple sky, but he could not shake her.

Had indulging his human side weakened him, as Cecilia had said? He raged as the peryton shook her mighty head, tossing him from side to side, as if he were a rival for her territory. With every whip of her body, Luca felt his strength waning. There was only one thing he could do. The Conjuror would have to wait.

I will endure.

Luca rocketed out over the western islands of Scotland until he was above open water. Grasping the peryton's antlers one more time, roaring at the shock of the cold, he flipped and plunged towards the rough water. The two of them shattered the surface of the sea in a torpedo of light.

45.

HUNGRY LIKE THE WOLF

On the cusp of the Cairngorms, Caravaggio shot out from behind the trees and up the steep hillside towards the cairn. At the same moment, a slavering two-headed hellhound bounded from the brush below in a cloud of mustard smoke, tearing up the hillside behind him.

'Draw, Matt!' Caravaggio yelled. '*Per l'amor di Dio*, draw!'

He was almost to the cairn. The hellhound's needle-sharp teeth snapped at his heels, the fiery jaws seconds from catching him.

Seconds were all that Matt needed. As the hound stood up on its hind legs, ready to attack, Matt fired a flaming white arrow directly into the soft valley between its two thick necks.

The hound howled. Two sets of jaws snapped at the arrow as it burned into the hairy flesh from arrow tip to feathery knock, driving deeper and deeper into the beast's core, the white flame burning the hound from within. The hound exploded in a single fiery flash.

Matt scrambled up the hill to Caravaggio, who was slapping his smoking, ruined boots against the ground. The artist's tunic was torn in places and one of the sleeves was hanging by a thread.

'I only just got these boots,' Caravaggio complained. 'I didn't want to lose them so soon. That was a bit too close for comfort, my friend. How did you know where to land your arrow?'

'It wasn't my first hellhound,' said Matt, helping the artist to his feet.

'Who set it on us?'

'Who set it on you I'd say.' Matt grimaced. 'Fire and brimstone at the church. A hellhound let loose. Someone's after your blood. Take an educated guess?'

Caravaggio whitened and spat on the ground. 'Luca Ferrante. How did that damn Nephilim know I was here?'

'That's what I'd like to know.'

Silently, the artist slid back down the hill with Matt side-stepping through the brush next to him. At the bottom, Caravaggio reached for a thick branch from the base of a nearby tree and pulled himself upright. Snapping off a low branch, he pivoted, thrusting the jagged end at Matt, who backed into a tree. Caravaggio flipped the stick and held it at Matt's throat, pinning him against the bark.

'You knew it was Luca,' he said. 'You let him set his hellhound on me. You wanted me to be killed, didn't you? No more trouble from the artist for you then, hmm?'

'What? You're mad!' protested Matt, struggling. 'Of course I didn't want him to get you. I had no idea Luca was tracking us.'

The artist pressed harder. His dark eyes were frightened. 'Don't keep anything like that from me again,' he hissed.

Matt shoved him away and stomped ahead, his brain racing, trying to sort out why Caravaggio's reaction had gone so quickly from fear to paranoia. He was hiding something. But what?

46.

FIRE AND BRIMSTONE

The sea was blazing like a burning oil slick where Luca and the peryton had plunged beneath the waves. Red and black streaked clouds crashed together in the unsettled and violent sky. The horizon was an inferno.

Rémy whirled about as a yellow Jeep tore across the lawn from the front of the Abbey, sending up sprays of muck with its wheels. It skidded to a halt, blocking their way into the house. Rémy's first instinct was to run, but by his side, Em was readying to fight.

The driver's side door flew open. A formidable looking man wearing a black untucked shirt, dark jeans shoved inside knee-high boots, leapt out. Em made an inarticulate sound and ran into his outstretched arms.

'Alessandro! I've never been so glad to see anyone in my life.'

Alessandro de Mendoza, known to his contemporaries in sixteenth-century Spain as the Moor of Cadiz and to Orion as the Professor, gathered Em into a warm embrace.

'Professor,' Rémy said, smiling as the man extended an arm to include Rémy in the hug. Although he knew these days that Alessandro was a noble soldier, a man of great fortune and a Guardian with fierce inspiriting powers, for Rémy he would forever be the old homeless scholar he had first met in London.

'What are you *doing* here?' Em gasped.

'I'll explain on the way.'

As if in agreement, thunder rumbled and cracked over the sea like colliding tectonic plates. Releasing them both, Alessandro opened the rear door of the Jeep and motioned for them to get in.

'We must get out of here,' he said.

'I have to get Mom's journal,' said Rémy. 'I left it inside when we were doing our research.'

Another crack of thunder shook the island. The fiery stain on the horizon brightened. A wave of fire hurtled into view, racing towards them. Alessandro started the Jeep and blasted the horn as Rémy raced into the house.

'Hurry!' Em screamed after him.

The book was on the kitchen table where he'd left it. He scooped it up and ran back outside. The edge of the fiery wave was already sweeping across the shore of the smaller island of Era Mina, setting fire to the thick brush on the beach before leaping into the narrow bay. The inferno would be on them in moments.

Alessandro yelled out the open window of the Jeep: 'Rémy! *Now*!'

The fire engulfed the boathouse and what was left of the dock. The flames seemed to pause for a moment, as if daring them to linger, as fingers of lava stretched towards the Jeep. The grass blackened, glowed and shrivelled beneath the tyres, and there was a smell of burning rubber.

Rémy jumped into the passenger side. Alessandro shifted gear and the Jeep sped away, bouncing down the driveway on its rims, hurtling towards the gates. Rémy heard a roar as the fire pounced on the walls of the Abbey behind them.

No one spoke until Alessandro was safely on the road, the Abbey glowed like a furnace in the distance.

'Do you think it survived?' Em asked quietly.

The Conjuror mark on Rémy's neck was swollen, and he rubbed it without thinking.

He knew she meant the peryton. 'I hope so. It saved us.'

Em was filthy. She had abrasions from slipping into the hole, a ton of tiny burns on her legs and arms from the falling ash, and a nasty cut under her thumb, but she was in one piece. Silently, Rémy thanked whichever gods were watching. He reached back and squeezed Em's hand. She squeezed back.

'That journal almost cost us our lives,' said Alessandro, watching Em outside animating new tyres on the Jeep.

The journal in Rémy's lap looked like a family recipe book. It bulged with scraps of paper covered in notes, fragments of sheet music and notations, torn pages from art gallery catalogues, and enough scribbled notes on napkins to open a diner. The flotsam and jetsam of Annie Dupree Rush's lifelong obsession with discovering the truth about Conjurors. For a long time, the journal had been Annie's lifeline to clarity and understanding, but she had died before finding the answers. It felt like a puzzle Rémy was trying to complete in darkness.

'It was worth the risk,' he said.

They passed a truck filled with volunteer firefighters from Seaport going the other way, sirens blaring and lights flashing. Alessandro turned up the hill behind Seaport and followed the winding road to the top of the island, cutting round the switchbacks on the narrow road. At the lookout point, he pulled to a stop and shut off the engine. Below them, a line of emergency vehicles were loading on to one of the Caledonian ferries while a Royal Coastguard helicopter scrambled into the angry sky from the station south of Largs.

'I thought we were getting off the island,' said Em in surprise. 'Not admiring the view.'

Alessandro smiled grimly.

'No reason why we can't do both,' he said.

LONDON

47.

TEA FOR THREE

The Kitten sisters, Violet and Anthea, lived in the three-storey Victorian mansion on Raphael Terrace in Knightsbridge that had been in their family since it was built. Their grandmother had been an inaugural member of the Women's Social and Political Union, and was one of the suffragettes to toss paint on future Prime Minister Winston Churchill when he was visiting their neighbours.

Much to the disgust of the same neighbours, the Kitten family had also run a soup kitchen and flop house for starving artists. Their work had brought them to Orion's attention, and the Kittens had been protectors and patrons of the Order of Era Mina ever since. The sisters were trusted and adored, their house an Orion safe-house known only to a select few in the organization.

The rear entrances to the houses on the terrace backed on to a mews that comprised garages and modern flats these days instead of stables. A rock star, three actors, and at least two members of the Royal family lived in the area, and security was tight if not always visible.

Vaughn waved at the camera installed above the Kittens' back door. From the top window of the house on the opposite corner, he spotted a flash of light and a figure watching him. One of the rock star's security details.

The door clicked and Vaughn pushed inside a clean, well-lit mudroom lined with brass hooks holding colourful raincoats, mud-stained gardening jackets, and one or two striped umbrellas. Four pairs of wellies stood at attention on a mat behind the door. The room had once been part of the stables, and the distinct smell of manure and wet hay still permeated the air.

'Vaughn darling,' called a bellowing voice from a speaker on the wall. Despite the danger they all were in, Vaughn relaxed at the sound of Violet's voice. 'Tea in the library.'

The route to the library took him along a wide hallway with floor-to-ceiling art by men and women who had at some time benefitted from Violet and Anthea's largesse. Vaughn's favourite was Paula Rego's portrait of the sisters in the mudroom after a day of gardening.

Anthea ushered him into the room, closing the door with the edge of her slipper. Violet's arthritis made standing a chore, so Vaughn bent and kissed her cheeks.

'We know this isn't a social visit,' said Violet, urging Vaughn to the empty chair.

'You look well,' said Anthea earnestly.

Violet passed Vaughn a plate of finger sandwiches. 'That's shite and you know it, Thea. He looks worn out and worried.'

Anthea glared. 'I was just trying to make small talk, Vi. Make Vaughn feel better. You want me to jump right in and say, "Have you averted the apocalypse yet?"'

Vaughn sipped his tea and ate a sandwich, trying not to laugh.

'So,' said Vi presently. '*Have* you averted the apocalypse?'

'Not yet.' He caught them up with the details about the explosions at the RA, the Abbey and Orion headquarters. 'We don't have the Bosch painting and the lyre either. I'm afraid we won't be able to control what we've set in motion.'

Violet patted his hand. 'Fear is only a monster. And fighting monsters is what we do best.'

'We do,' Vaughn conceded. 'But the Camarilla's monsters are much more seductive than they used to be. This isn't going to be a four-horsemen-destroy-the-world kind of apocalypse. It will be much more insidious. And it's already started. Government coups, mass genocide, civil wars, social revolutions, industry takeovers, banks failing. It all appears organic, but it isn't. It's part of their plan. The Camarilla will be impossible to stop when the Watchers rise.'

Anthea looked concerned. 'How did we let this happen?'

'The Camarilla has raised an army of foot soldiers among our kind,' said Vaughn. 'They are promising them the world and more.'

'I thought we'd wiped out the last of the Camarilla bastards in the Second World War,' said Violet, topping up her cup. 'It sounds as if I was wrong.'

Vaughn brushed the crumbs from his jeans and got to his feet. He embraced them both before returning to the mudroom. He removed one of the gardening jackets from its hook, the jacket Anthea was wearing in the Rego portrait, and turned the hook beneath it twice, clockwise. The wall slid open and Vaughn stepped inside a steel enclosed panic room where a painting that never failed to make him thirsty was displayed, Édouard Manet's *A Bar at the Folies-Bergère*.

The wall closed, plunging him into darkness. The only illumination in the room came from a tennis ball of light rippling above the painting.

Someone was already inside.

48.

MIND YOUR MANETS

Vaughn faded into the Manet, landing gracefully on the black marble floor. The room was packed with rich men in top hats and bohemian women in fashionable gowns. Two courtesans in feather boas looked up from drinking absinthe at a nearby table.

'Your entrances are always elegant,' said one.

'I aim to please,' said Vaughn, bowing.

'You'll want the corner booth,' said the other.

Before Vaughn could sit down, Zach had slid out of the booth and was embracing him.

Vaughn returned the love. 'Glad to see you, mate,' he signed, slapping Zach's back as they settled back into the booth.

Zach Butler was one of the toughest young men Vaughn knew, with imaginative power unique to his abilities in coding and design. Under his father Simon's tutelage, Zach had achieved more than anyone could have predicted on Orion's behalf.

'And your mother?' Vaughn wondered how best to phrase his question. 'How is she?'

Zach's smile dimmed a little. He'd recently discovered that his mother hadn't died when he was a baby, but had gone deep undercover for Orion instead. The two of them had reunited recently, but it had been hard.

'She's fine,' he signed after a moment. 'We're both fine.'

Vaughn saw the conflict cross Zach's expression. Along with being abandoned by Em, the love of his life, during the Guardian ceremony, Zach had been processing the fact that his mother had abandoned him too. Orianna Butler had been one of Orion's most prized assets for almost twenty years, hidden deep undercover in the ranks of the Camarilla and now he was working undercover with her.

'She isn't expecting to be forgiven for abandoning me,' continued Zach. 'In fact, she doesn't expect anything from me at all.'

'Under the circumstances that's a good thing,' signed Vaughn.

'It is.' Zach paused. 'But I feel like she should *want* me to forgive her.'

'Don't push it,' added Vaughn, shaking out flecks of paint from his hair. 'She's more complicated than most of us.'

'How's Dad?'

'Fine. Worried about you. Trying not to show it.'

'Give him my love. I miss him. I miss everyone.'

Vaughn could see that Zach was desperate to ask about Em, but his pride wouldn't let him. He fidgeted with a button on his sleeve instead, before placing his hands flat on the table. Vaughn tactfully changed the subject.

'Who knew you'd develop your own distinctive Animare abilities?' he said. 'I'm so proud of you.'

Zach returned Vaughn's smile, and for the first time in many months, looked more like his old self. 'Must've been all the William Gibson I read.'

'Your mum had something to do with it too.' Vaughn sat back against the leather booth, wanting to say much more, but knowing this wasn't the time. 'It's great to see you Zach, but contacting me was risky. You need to be in Rome, especially now Luca has the Bosch painting and the lyre.'

'The Camarilla doesn't trust Luca at the moment.' Zach's fingers were a blur. 'They have him on a tight leash.'

'The Camarilla doesn't trust its own Nephilim? Fancy that.'

'The Camarilla doesn't trust anyone. Ever since Cecilia Ciardi took control, she's been erratic and quick to anger. They know we've infiltrated them. And they're moving more quickly than ever.' Zach flexed his fingers and studied his palms briefly before resuming. 'You saw Cecilia's announcement about the concert at St Peter's Square tomorrow?'

Vaughn nodded. 'It's why Jeannie's decided to move matters on.'

The female bartender brought them both a pink frothy drink in a martini glass. Vaughn sipped it, and made a face. 'Jesus, that tastes like turpentine.'

'Probably is,' signed Zach. 'I contacted you because two things have come up that we haven't planned for.'

'What?'

'First, Callum Muir. Do you know him?'

'The Earl of Dundonal's son?' Vaughn rubbed the shadow of a beard on his face. 'The Muir family have been patrons of Era Mina since the Middle Ages. What about his son?'

'I saw Cecilia talking about him with one of her lieutenants. Callum Muir stole a map from the Keats-Shelley Museum and replaced it with a forgery. Cecilia was furious. She wants the original back. Fiera Orsini asked me to get him out of Rome. I may need to bring him to Raphael Terrace for a while.'

Vaughn considered the problem. 'Are you sure you can do that without compromising your position with Cecilia? I need you to stay near her until this is over.'

'She's watching everyone closely, but I think I can get him here without too much trouble. He's safely snoring at the Villa Orsini right now.'

'You've already risked your life to get inside the Camarilla and reconnect with your mother,' Vaughn said, suddenly wishing he hadn't asked. 'I couldn't bear it if anything happened to you.' He put his hand on Zach's. 'If it's getting too dangerous, come home. We can monitor Luca and the Camarilla through Orianna.'

'I'm not quitting,' signed Zach, annoyed, pulling away.

Vaughn sighed, torn between pride and fear. 'You said there were two things. What else?'

'Cecilia murdered her banker. Cut the guy's head off.' Zach's sleeve slid up his wrist, revealing his Camarilla tattoo. 'It was brutal. She's never got her hands dirty before. She's getting paranoid.'

'Which banker?' asked Vaughn sharply, afraid of the answer.

'Victor,' signed Zach. He grimaced. 'It was Victor.'

'Ah, shit.' Vaughn rubbed his face again. Victor Moretti had been an Orion informant for years. 'What about Victor's family?'

'Orianna got them safely to Switzerland, but somehow Cecilia found out they'd fled.'

Vaughn wanted to kick the table. 'She's ramping up to something big if she's cleaning house. It's going to happen at the concert. No doubt about it. Are you sure your cover's safe?'

'For now.' After a beat, Zach added: 'Victor didn't expose us. And Cecilia seems to still trust my mum.'

'And you came through with Luca, so there's that too. It was a relief to get your text about his agreement yesterday.'

Zach slid from the booth, but Vaughn grabbed his hand.

'Right now, we can't trust anyone,' he said. 'Take care, son.'

'Take care yourself.'

SCOTLAND

49.

TAKING THE HIGH ROAD

'I am glad you are both unhurt,' said Alessandro de Mendoza.

The Moor spoke several Romance and African languages but because he'd learned his English at the Spanish court in the 1520s and 1530s, his intonation was crisp and his constructions a little antiquated.

'I hope the improvement in the weather means the peryton survived,' said Em, picking at the dried blood on her palm as she gazed out across the bay. The sky above Auchinmurn was thickening with smoke, but the thunder had stopped and the clouds were breaking up.

Rémy set his hand on the Moor's broad forearm. 'How many times have you saved my life now?'

'I am not inclined to keep count.'

The scar running across Alessandro's eyebrow from his battle with the Inquisitor centuries ago gave the impression he was about to wink, but Em sensed that was far from the reality.

'You two were lucky I arrived when I did.' His expression darkened to something explosive. 'What in the name of all that is holy did you think you were doing, leaving the safe-house in Glasgow? You were given *explicit* instructions to stay.'

'We were getting on each other's nerves,' Rémy said.

Alessandro gave an unamused smile. 'Ah, well, that's reasonable.' He slammed his hand so hard on the armrest that Em and Rémy both jumped. 'Much better to be captured by a Nephilim than be annoyed by each other.'

Em exchanged a startled glance with Rémy. 'You know it was Luca who blew up the Abbey?'

'Yes! And *you* weren't meant to be there.'

That was a strange thing to say, Em thought. Did the Moor know it was going to happen?

'I don't suppose you know where your brother and the artist are hiding?' Alessandro inquired. 'We are still trying to find them.'

Em's skin prickled. She hadn't thought about Matt or Caravaggio for hours. She and Rémy had barely escaped. What if her brother hadn't been so lucky? She closed her eyes, trying to feel him out.

'Can you sense him?' Rémy asked her, suddenly alert by her side.

'We're too far apart for telepathy.' Nerves made Em bite the side of her thumb. 'But I'm pretty sure they went to Orion HQ, near Kentigern.'

Alessandro looked grim. 'That is gone too,' he said. 'Under orders from the Camarilla, the Nephilim hit the Royal Academy, then the Kentigern vault directly before he came here, right after stealing Bosch's *Garden of Earthly Delights* last night from the Prado.'

Em bit her thumb so hard that she drew blood. *Matt, where are you? Are you safe?*

'The Kentigern vault imploded,' Alessandro went on. 'No bodies were found. That would suggest to me that your brother and the artist are still alive.'

'Sounds like there's a but coming,' said Rémy.

Tension deepened the lines on Alessandro's face. 'But Orion found evidence of a violent confrontation in the forest above the compound.'

The Royal Coastguard helicopter broke through the clouds in a swirl of hot air and whooping blades. Alessandro looked up.

'Come,' he said. 'Our carriage is here. We are going back to Glasgow, where you should have been all this time.'

Em sensed a rush of emotion from Rémy. She even glimpsed images: his mother dying on a small kitchen floor, his aunt lying wounded in his arms. She moved instinctively towards him before he had even opened his mouth.

'I'm not going.' Rémy's voice was loud and firm over the sound of the descending helicopter. 'I mean it. I'm tired of the noises in my head. Tired of the grip the

Inquisitor and his Camarilla have on my life, my future. I'm not going to Glasgow.

'I'm going back to Rome. This ends with me.'

50.

TAKING THE LOW ROAD

I t took Matt and Caravaggio twenty minutes to hobble into the Caledonia Rangers Station, one barefoot carrying a dagger in leather trousers and torn shirt with a handful of scratches across his back, the other with long hair loose and curly wearing sunglasses and carrying a sketchpad.

'Well, now,' said the elderly ranger in surprise. 'If you two aren't a sight fer sare eyes.'

Caravaggio gave his most charming smile. 'We're comrades in arms who have got into difficulties on the mountain. Can you assist us with clothing and the like?'

'Aye, right,' said the ranger, rolling his eyes and stepping to a display case with plaid shirts and Scottish National Trust hoodies for sale. He grabbed a large sweatshirt and tossed it to Caravaggio. 'Put this on. Ye can pay me later.'

'Thanks,' said Matt, pulling his hair away from his face. 'But we really need a phone.'

The ranger eyed them. 'Yer from that hippy commune in the auld kirk, I bet?'

'It's not a hippy commune,' said Matt. 'It's an artists' colony.'

The ranger snorted. 'Aye and I'm Bonnie Prince Charlie.'

'I met him once,' said Caravaggio.

'Shut up,' said Matt, glaring at Caravaggio. 'Might we use your phone, sir?'

The ranger lifted an old-fashioned dial phone and set it on the counter in front of Matt. Matt frowned at it.

'It's no like it's a telegraph, son,' the ranger prompted. 'It works fine.'

On a desk at the back of the hut, a shortwave radio crackled.

'HQ to Ranger Station Five. HQ to Ranger Station Five. Geordie, are you there? We've got a situation at the auld kirk. I repeat, we have a situation.'

The ranger gaped at the radio, then whirled around.

'Don't move,' he squeaked, fumbling for the radio at his side. 'Either of ye. Or I'll have yer brains for mince!'

'Lovely sentiment,' said Caravaggio, leaning on the counter. 'Leave the heavy lifting to me, Matt.'

The artist picked up the heavy phone and heaved it at the ranger. It hit the man on the head and sent him sprawling to the ground.

'But I hadn't called Em,' Matt protested as Caravaggio seized his arm.

'That's gratitude,' the artist grumbled. 'I just saved us from the noose. You twenty-first century boys don't have a clue when trouble comes knocking.'

'They don't hang people in the twenty-first century.'

'Shut up and move,' instructed Caravaggio, pushing Matt out of the ranger's hut. 'His compatriots will be here at any moment when the old fool doesn't call in.'

They climbed to the top of the hill as swiftly as they could, and hid behind a row of thick pines and fir trees, checking the way was clear.

When they stepped out onto the gravel road, Matt was already drawing, his fingers flying across the page. He put one or two finishing touches to his animation, then he turned his attention to drawing another pair of boots for Caravaggio.

'Do you know how to ride this mechanized beast?' said Caravaggio, walking with some trepidation around the motorcycle Matt had animated.

'Vaughn taught all of us to drive one before we were old enough to drive anything else,' Matt explained as Caravaggio ran his hands over the double seat. 'Put these on.' He tossed over a leather jacket, chaps, and a helmet from the pile he'd animated.

'I'd rather watch you,' said Caravaggio, holding up the chaps and grinning.

'Glad you're back to your usual self.'

Matt grabbed the chaps and tugged them over his jeans, zipped the leather jacket, and fastened his helmet, tucking his curly hair underneath. He straddled the motorcycle and started its engine, which coughed a couple of times before it caught. Caravaggio fastened his helmet too and climbed behind Matt, wrapping his arms round his waist.

'Where are we going?' Caravaggio shouted over the roar of the engine, as Matt guided the motorcycle cautiously along the single file lane towards the main junction and the road to Perth.

'To find Em and Rémy!'

51.

PROTECT AND SERVE

'The last time the Camarilla orchestrated something world-changing was during the Inquisition in the sixteenth century,' said Alessandro shifting expertly up the Haylie Brae and away from Largs. 'They then made two serious attempts during both World Wars.'

Rémy's eyes were closed and despite the low thrumming in his head, his mind was tuned to every word. Em was listening too.

'Their grip is stronger now than it has ever been and their reach is far. Too many strange and unsettling events are occurring in the world lately to ignore.' The Moor cut out in front of a lorry and flew past it, pulling back in and speeding up over ninety.

'When did you learn to drive so well?' asked Em.

'I can't remember,' said Alessandro. 'My memory fragments sometimes. I lose whole loops of time the longer I stay out of my portrait and in the world.'

'Why did you decide to send the helicopter away?' asked Rémy.

'You already know of my oath to protect Conjurors, Rémy,' said the Moor. His mouth twisted. 'Part of the arrangement includes following their whims, however dangerous.' He glanced in the rear-view mirror. 'I do not wish to control you. Merely protect.'

He shifted down as they slowed through a small village where they stopped to go to the bathroom, get petrol and grab some crisps and chocolate. They were back on the A737 in less than fifteen minutes, with Rémy scarfing down a large bag of Thai-flavoured crisps and Em a Galaxy bar.

'How many Animare and Guardians are working with the Camarilla here in Britain?' asked Em, popping a square of chocolate in her mouth.

'Too many,' said Alessandro. 'They have extended their reach into every profession, but into politics especially, nurturing dictatorships and democracies alike. What exactly were you hoping to find in the Abbey's library that was worth risking your lives?'

'We were trying to find out more about the prophecy depicted in the frieze in Luca's tomb, the Tomb of the Martyrs,' Rémy said. 'You know, the wall where I'm being crowned with laurels. I want to go back in time, to see when it was carved. Matt can...' He paused, wondering how much to tell Alessandro of Matt's historical vision abilities.

'Use his eyes to see into the past?'

Em and Rémy exchanged glances. Of course, he knew.

Alessandro crossed over the M8 and followed the signs for airport rental parking. 'If you could see this happen,' he said, 'you think you could understand the prophecy? You think you could change the destiny etched in that stone that suggests you are a king?'

'Dumb idea, I guess,' said Rémy, slumping back in his seat.

'Dumb indeed,' said Alessandro. 'The last place you should be is Rome, Rémy. Trust me.'

52.

EYES ON THE PAST

Hours after passing through Perth, Matt drove the motorbike on to the grassy verge among a copse of trees at the top of the Haylie Brae and shut off the engine.

'Are we there yet?' said the artist, pulling off his helmet, his hair sticking out of his ponytail in stiff clumps.

'No.'

He jogged across the field bordering the A90 at the peak of the Brae. The long grass was still damp from the storm earlier in the day, and Matt's trousers and chaps were soaked by the time he reached the peak and gazed out over the isle of Auchinmurn and its smaller sister island: two puzzle pieces floating in Largs Bay. He swore under his breath.

'What in God's name is that?' said Caravaggio, catching up, breathless and staring.

The entire southern edge of Auchinmurn was glowing with a helix of blues, pinks, and oranges spinning up from a palpitating black vortex. The 3D shape reminded Matt of a design from a Spirograph.

In the middle of the bay, the returning Caledonian ferry had a fire engine and an emergency responder's Jeep on the parking deck. Matt could see the glint of cameras filming the strange borealis effect. He pulled his sketchpad from his inside pocket, animating binoculars in swift strokes of light. Then he yanked Caravaggio behind the cover of a border of gorse bushes and focused the binoculars. He groaned, dropped the binoculars and dipped his head to rest between his knees. Caravaggio squeezed his shoulder.

Em! Where are you? he called, from deep in his mind.

There was no response. Just a dull echo, as if Em had faded somewhere out of his reach. He sympathized. It's what he would have done, given the choice.

'I am sure they're fine,' said Caravaggio.

Matt glanced at him. 'Are you?'

Caravaggio shrugged. 'No.'

Matt rubbed his eyes, trying to think. 'Give me a second.'

He stood up, cracked his knuckles and rolled his neck muscles, blinking rapidly until his eyes began to water and his hands started fading from his vision. He took up the binoculars again, concentrating on the island, letting time rewind. It only worked when significant events in the past had left distinct traces on a particular place. But God knows, the two islands and this part of Scotland had seen their share of significance and the supernatural.

At first all Matt could see were the colours in the gyre brightening. Then his eyes began to absorb the light. The helix spun faster, the colours blending. Matt's body temperature was dropping as his energy shifted in his imagination.

The present rewound in front of Matt's eyes – Luca in his flawless form launching a fiery projectile at the abbey's tower, Em forcing her bloody hand into the earth, the majestic peryton dropping from a shimmer in the sky. He watched until he saw Em and Rémy's escape. Only then did he close his eyes.

GLASGOW

53.

WHITE WEDDING

In the empty car park behind the Kelvingrove Art Gallery in Glasgow, the sky was a deep purple and there was a chill in the wind. Matt parked the bike in the shadows of a shed at the edge of the walking path. He wouldn't get rid of it just yet.

Caravaggio stared up at the red sandstone building with wide eyes. With its multiple spires and austere detailing, it stood on the border of Kelvingrove Park looking down on Glasgow's west-end like a prim aunt. 'It looks like a Dutch palace,' he said in admiration. 'So this is the place where you and Em first hid me from Orion?'

Matt nodded while he punched in the security code. The smaller of the two doors on the dock clicked open. 'Orion uses it as a base in the city, so we have security clearance. Plus it's encrypted. The log won't show us having come through here.'

At the doors into the main gallery, Matt tapped in another code. Caravaggio was about to push through when Matt held him back.

'Wait.'

'What?'

'It's a rolling key. The door first, then the alarms in the galleries.'

They walked past the early Impressionists, heading towards the gallery displaying art from the Glasgow Boys. Suddenly, Caravaggio took off in the opposite direction.

'Wait!' Matt chased behind the artist down the hallway. 'We need to leave Glasgow, we don't have time for sightseeing.'

He caught up with Caravaggio in an exhibit titled, 'Brueghel and the Art of the Crowd'. Pieter Brueghel the Elder's *The Peasant Wedding* was the featured painting. It showed the inside of a cottage, wedding guests sitting at a crowded banquet table while beer was poured in abundance. Two pipers accompanied the celebration.

The artist's hand was whipping across a blank page in his sketchbook while he kept his eye on the painting in front of him.

'Please tell me you have a good reason for this,' said Matt, crossly.

A thin skein of light ballooned out from Caravaggio's page. 'We will leave Glasgow shortly,' Caravaggio murmured as he drew. 'But first, we will replenish our bodies and our souls.'

Matt sighed. He'd spent enough time around the artist to know his chances of convincing him to change his mind were slim. Besides, he was hungry and exhausted by his efforts at Auchinmurn. If he'd heeded one lesson from his grandfather over the years, it was that fading from one painting to another is dangerous if your imagination is depleted.

He took a deep breath, stepped inside the mushrooming light and put his hand on Caravaggio's hip. Together, they crashed a wedding.

54.

TROUBLE FROM YOUR KIND

The father of the bride glared from beneath his black skull cap while two of the wedding guests mumbled to each other across the corner of the table. The piper in the foreground had spotted them as they faded, and had a wary eye on them as he played his jig. But for the most part, the peasants in the painting ignored the two interlopers.

Caravaggio lifted a jug from a basket in the foreground of the canvas and held it in front of a ginger-haired man pouring the beer. The man looked doubtfully at him.

'Will you be staying?'

'We'll stay long enough to get drunk and eat our fill,' said Caravaggio cheerfully. 'Then we'll be off.'

The man gave him an icy stare. 'Had enough trouble from your kind already. Drink up and be gone with you.'

The heat from the revellers, the low drone of the bagpipes and Matt's exhaustion were conspiring against him. He yawned and took a slug of beer. The drink was sweet and rich, tasting more like a full-bodied cider than an ale or beer, and he felt a little better for it. His brain caught up with what the barman had said.

'Animare have been through here before,' he said slowly.

'And who can blame them?' said Caravaggio, taking a hearty draught of beer. 'We are all entitled to ale, sex and song when we travel.'

'But this isn't a travel painting,' Matt pointed out. 'There's no art we can use inside here. You and I are not going anywhere but back to the Kelvingrove gallery. Why would another Animare visit this place?'

'For ale, sex and song,' Caravaggio said patiently. 'Why else?'

Matt scratched behind the ears of a white dog scavenging for scraps under the table. He gently nudged the dog away from the legs and the sword of the wealthy merchant nearby.

'*Goedenavond*,' said Matt courteously to the merchant as he helped himself to a bowl of soup. It tasted of wet brown paper. 'Have you had trouble from other travellers like us recently?'

'We rarely see your kind,' said the merchant, regarding him a little fearfully. '*Bezelien*. But that one,' he nodded towards Caravaggio, 'he's been here before. He likes the ale, and the company. Last time he brought a present for the bride and groom.'

'What did he bring?'

'A violin.'

'Really,' said Matt thoughtfully. He set his plate of broth on the ground for the dog and looked around for Caravaggio. The artist was making his way back towards him. He looked pleased with himself.

'Fetch the next round of ale, Matt, my darling.'

Matt grabbed Caravaggio by the collar. 'Listen, you smug Italian bastard. The smell of piss and pig shit are suffocating in here. Stop lying and tell me why you presented a violin of all things to the bride and groom last time you were here.'

With a dark look in his eyes Caravaggio gulped the last of his ale. 'Brueghel's are a favourite of mine. When you left me here a while back, I got bored. I did some bar hopping.' The artist detached himself irritably from Matt's grip and wiped his mouth with his sleeve.

'And the violin?'

'A man must pay his debts.'

55.

UNDER CONSTRUCTION

After fading back into the Kelvingrove gallery, Matt marched ahead trying to make sense of why not that long ago Caravaggio had been fading with a violin.

'Are we leaving now?' Caravaggio inquired as they hurried back through the museum corridors.

'I need access to the internet first,' said Matt, walking to the stairs.

'That interesting library on your computer device?'

In the museum's office suite, Caravaggio settled down for a nap while Matt logged in to the Orion database through the local network. An 'Under Construction' screen came up. He tried again. Same thing. He took off his jacket and refreshed the screen. The user of this computer had the *Guardian* news page on view. The first headline took Matt's breath away.

'Michele, you have to see this.' Matt picked up a magazine from the desk, rolled it up and threw it at the artist's head.

In one swift move, Caravaggio was on his feet, knife drawn. '*Che diavolo...*'

'There's been an explosion at the RA in London.'

They both stared at an image from a news helicopter of the black hole at the east wing of the Royal Academy.

'The Council Chamber,' said Matt. Fear gripped his throat. 'Jeannie and Vaughn are there.'

'Orion headquarters, Auchinmurn Abbey *and* the Council Chamber?' said Caravaggio. 'This is bad news, my friend.'

Matt read on. 'They're blaming a gas leak. No loss of life or any serious injuries. But the press wouldn't know about the Council Chamber...' He leaned back in the desk chair, trying not to panic. 'It explains why the Orion database is down. We're in damage control.'

Caravaggio struck the down arrow as if the key had offended his honour. 'This is all Luca Ferrante,' he growled. 'He attacked Orion HQ. You saw him attack the Abbey with your crazy eyes. And now he has hit the Council Chamber as well.'

'Three places at about the same time. How is that even possible?' Matt asked, struggling to understand.

'Time is a human construct,' Caravaggio pointed out. 'And Luca's not human.'

56.

PICASSO BABY

When Animare had first banded together with Guardians for protection during the Middle Ages, a painting within another painting was uncommon. And so during the Renaissance the most powerful of Animare took it upon themselves to create 'gallery paintings', through which they could travel. From then on, prominent Animare in each period had created one or two travel paintings. Vermeer had been the most prolific. One of Orion's first assignments on behalf of the Order of Era Mina had been to build an international database of these travel paintings.

Matt opened the database. It looked like a subway map, except instead of images of stations, thumbnails of the paintings appeared. Three options to get to London lit up the screen. The first route involved a Turner painting of the sea.

'Avoid that one,' advised Caravaggio. 'I'd rather not get wet.'

'What about your old friend, James Guthrie?' Matt suggested. 'His painting here in the Kelvingrove gets us directly to Tate Britain in London.'

'Must we?'

'I thought you two got along fine when you last visited.'

Caravaggio sighed. 'Oh we did.'

Matt caught a whiff of deception in Caravaggio's response, but he didn't have time to dwell on it. They needed to get to London and find Em and Remy.

They headed through contemporary art towards the Guthrie paintings. Caravaggio was struggling to focus, marvelling as they went.

'What the devil is that?' he said as they passed an angular painting full of colour.

'A modernist work,' said Matt, towing him on. 'You wouldn't like it in there. Your body would be rebuilt in triangular fragments and your legs and feet would be all wrong. There's a reason Picasso and his like aren't on the travel maps.'

Inside Guthrie's *Hard At It*, they ducked under the artist's white umbrella. When Guthrie saw Matt, he handed him a note.

'It's from Em,' said Matt.

We're at the Professor's. Come quickly.

LONDON

57.

DOWNTOWN TRAIN

The evening's trains running underground from Charing Cross station shook Alessandro de Mendoza's lair. The vibrations took a while to adjust to.

'It's been my home for many years,' Alessandro told Em and Rémy as they each took a seat in the abandoned World War Two air-raid shelter deep under the city. 'The regular tremors of the tiled walls gave a rhythm to my life that I have welcomed.'

A rattling knocked a stack of tattered paperback mysteries and an empty plastic water jug onto the filthy concrete at Em's feet.

'Northern Line,' Alessandro remarked. 'Are you sure your brother and the artist will come?'

'They'll be here,' Em said confidently.

Almost before she had finished speaking, Matt and Caravaggio ducked into the Professor's underground lair.

'Sorry, got here as fast as we could,' said Matt a little breathlessly as Em hugged him tight and Rémy clapped him on the back.

'A happy gathering, I see.'

Em ran to hug Vaughn, who had appeared under the blue tarp that covered the entrance to the shelter. He was carrying an M&S shopping bag packed with food and drink.

'I came as soon as I got your message that everyone would be here, Alessandro.' Vaughn released Em, ruffled Matt's hair and nodded to Rémy. 'But if you ever disobey my orders again, I'll bind you myself. What the hell were you thinking? You weren't supposed to be there. You could all have been killed.'

That was the second time Em had heard that expression in as many hours.

'Why do I get the feeling you and Alessandro know more than you're letting on?' she said.

In the following silence, Caravaggio lifted a packet of M&S sandwiches from Vaughn's bag and removed the cellophane. 'Modern cuisine,' he said through a mouthful. 'It's a marvel.'

Vaughn nodded at Alessandro.

'Orion knew Luca was coming,' Alessandro began. 'He took out the Royal Academy as well as Kentigern and Auchinmurn. But as we have said, *you* weren't supposed to be there. None of you.'

There was a long silence.

'Orion *let* Luca destroy the vaults and the Royal Academy?' echoed Em at last, her voice faint.

Vaughn sighed. 'We knew the Camarilla was planning an attack. We decided to let it play out, to let them think we are no longer a threat to their final plans.'

'But Rémy and I almost *died*! And the art...' Em's voice shook. 'Jeannie was at the Royal Academy, at the Council meeting. Is she all right?'

'Jeannie is fine,' said Vaughn shortly. 'We took a risk, OK? In our defence, none of you should've been anywhere near the vaults. You all should have been in the Glasgow safe-house.'

'We saw him do it. Me and Rémy. And the peryton...' Em trailed away. She hoped the peryton had survived the battle.

'I saw him too,' Matt said quietly, fiddling with his sunglasses. 'But now that I'm thinking about what happened, he could have taken us out. Instead, he unleashed a hellhound to chase us off like he was playing with us.'

'Listen,' said Vaughn, dumping out the bag onto the makeshift table, 'after what happened at the Castel Sant'Angelo Jeannie and I decided that if we wanted to stop the Camarilla once and for all, we needed to know where the portal is located and destroy it, and to do that we needed to let the Camarilla believe that we are no longer a threat.'

Rémy rubbed his hands over his head. 'Let me get

this straight. You're saying that the only way to find the portal and destroy it is to let the Camarilla open it first?'

Vaughn glanced at Alessandro before nodding.

'Wait,' said Em, her anger rising, 'what do you have planned next? Are you going to just give them Rémy and the sacred chord?'

Alessandro straightened up to face Em's anger. 'Of course not, the sacred chord remains safe in the Duke of Albion's vault, but we have always thought the Camarilla had other means to its endgame. All we did was remove a few obstacles to see what would happen—'

'And when we knew Luca was wavering in his support of the Camarilla, we had to take the chance to bring him to our side,' Vaughn cut in.

'We're playing nice with a Nephilim too?' said Em, thinking of the powerful Nephilim, of the damage he'd wreaked on the Abbey. She thought about the battle at Castel Sant'Angelo, and those terrible moments deep underground in Rome. Luca Ferrante: the enemy. Luca Ferrante: the friend. Either way he was dangerous.

'We are,' said Vaughn. 'Or we're trying to, but then Luca stole Bosch's tryptich.'

'That's where the lyre's hidden,' said Rémy.

Vaughn nodded. 'We have to assume he knows the lyre is in the third panel, and hope he gives it to us, and not to the other side.'

Caravaggio stood up. 'You are such fools. Of course, he'll give the lyre to the Camarilla, and then he'll come for me and exact his revenge for my part in Sebina's death.'

'Sit down, Michele,' ordered Alessandro. 'Eat. It'll keep your mouth busy.'

Matt pulled his hair back from his face. 'I just have one question.'

'What?' said Vaughn.

'How does Orion know so much about what's happening inside the Camarilla in Rome?'

Vaughn glanced at Em before answering. 'Because Zach is undercover at the highest level of the Camarilla.'

Em dropped her glass. It shattered on the hard concrete floor, and it was several moments before the space quietened.

'Are you kidding me,' howled Em. 'The bastard turned my hair to snakes in Chicago. I haven't forgotten.'

Vaughn's face was expressionless. 'Zach is on our side. For what it's worth, it killed him to hurt you.'

'I bet it did,' Em snapped.

'Snakes in the head in return for a snake in his heart,' chided Caravaggio.

'He and his mom did save me from suffocating in the Titian painting,' said Rémy, trying to diffuse the tension. He sat on the edge of Alessandro's bunk. 'But if Luca gives the Camarilla the lyre—'

'Does the Pope wear a hat?' said Caravaggio under his breath.

'—then Alessandro's right. They must have another way to open the portal to Chaos and bring forth the Watchers.'

Alessandro stepped in front of Rémy who was flipping through Annie's journal. 'What are you thinking?'

'That we need to find another way, too.'

58.

SOUND AND VISION

Another train rumbled overhead, knocking a bottle of whisky from its cardboard shelf. Caravaggio lunged and caught it before it crashed to the concrete. 'That would have been a damn shame,' he said.

Rémy was buried in his mom's journal, anxiety etched across his brow while Matt was reading one of Alessandro's paperbacks in the corner, and Vaughn was stretched on the bunk with his eyes closed, thinking. Alessandro was pacing in front of Rémy.

'What happened to the boy you rescued from the Inquisitor in Spain all those years ago, Alessandro?' asked Em, sitting next to Rémy and trying not to dwell on the news about Zach. 'You've never told us much about him.'

'His name was Cadjo,' said Alessandro quietly. 'But that's another story for another time. *Some secrets are ours to keep.*'

'*Musica vivificat mortuos,*' Em said absently.

The irritation faded from Rémy's expression. 'Why did you say that? That phrase is everywhere in my mom's journal.'

Em held Rémy's startled gaze. 'It just came into my head when Alessandro was talking. Last time I was in the Jacob Lawrence painting, recovering from Zach's snake attack by the way, the phrase was on the mirror on the wall.'

'You must have caught the tail of my memory,' said Alessandro, sadness clouding his eyes. 'Cadjo learned the phrase from his family. I taught him how to say it in Latin. It became our motto of sorts.'

A sudden blast of energy hit Em from the Professor, flashing a series of rippling images like a flip book in her imagination. She grabbed a sketchpad and pencil from the table and started to draw, her fingers sketching furiously, the heel of her hand shading and smudging, her imagination creating a faint halo of light above the page. Nothing animated. She was in control. After a few minutes, breathless, she sat back, her cheeks rosy red, a thin sheen of sweat on her forehead.

'I just saw this in your head, Alessandro,' she said.

She had animated the images in a series of panels, each one moving the way she'd seen them in her mind, each panel drawn in a photographic detail that was astonishing. One after the other they rose a few centimetres off the surface, like a comic in 3D. The images showed an underwater shipwreck with the trunk of a tree growing through the middle of the deck, its branches shooting out through iron manacles that waved in the water like limbs. Starting in the second panel and running the rest of the page, the tree transformed into an angel with brown skin, black eyes, and gold-flecked wings rising out of the murky depths. The angel was playing a pitch pipe.

Alessandro stared at it fascinated. 'In the slave markets in Seville, I heard men and women tell of such an angel and a lost ship. It must have come into my mind when I was speaking of Cadjo. I believe your mum wrote of it in her journal.' He glanced at Rémy. 'It was the ship that carried your ancestor, the first Conjuror to the Americas.'

Alessandro closed his eyes and placed his hands together against his lips. A train trundled along a nearby tunnel, breaking the silence with the screech of its airbrakes. Everything in the lair shook again.

'The story began like this,' Alessandro said after a moment. 'When this ship sailed from Seville, the men and women left standing on the blocks began to chant. The chant became a song so beautiful it brought tears to everyone's eyes. I asked an old woman chained to an iron stake on the dusty ground what the song was about. She told me it was a lamentation, a song for the dead. The ship was doomed. I asked her how she knew that. She said because the devil was on board.'

*

Without understanding why, the music filled Rémy's mind as Alessandro described it. A song, pure and perfect and magical. He heard his mom singing in his head, saw her dancing across the cracked linoleum of their Chicago kitchen, the room ablaze in light, her voice rising to a crescendo that had brought a young Rémy to his knees. With the song still sounding in his head, he flipped through the journal's middle pages. 'My mom noted multiple versions that the Dupree women told each other down the centuries about how the first Conjuror came to America. Ah, here it is.'

Rémy cleared his throat.

'"The first Conjuror came to America in a slave ship. In 1797 a lone ship drifted up a tributary of the Mississippi. Alonzo Blue, overseer of the Dupree Plantation, spotted the two-decker bobbing in the choppy water. As word spread of the ship's strange arrival, the field slaves vanished into their damp huts, closed their shutters and shoved pellets of hardtack into their ears. It was as if they knew what was coming."'

'Alonzo Blue eventually took over the plantation,' he explained, looking up from the journal. 'He's another ancestor of mine.'

Em nudged him. 'Keep reading.'

Rémy did.

'"Then at dusk the voice of an angel singing a wordless aria could be heard, like the fluting sound of the breeze through the sugar cane, or the delicate notes of the harpsichord in the big house's front parlour. The music floated from the ship in a pulsing silver mist, above the moss-draped oaks, through the rubber trees dripping with wet lichen, dipping and darting across the indigo fields until it reached the party at the plantation house, where handsome guests were sipping sweetened rum from tulip-shaped glasses on the wide veranda.

At the cool touch of the mist, the guests' fingers twitched, their limbs stiffened, their eyes fluttered and their glasses fell to the wooden planks of the porch. The women's ears trickled blood on to the lace of their white cotton dresses. The men's collars sliced into the throbbing veins in their necks. Only then did the music stop."'

Rémy paused to catch his breath. 'I could never figure out the next part. It's a series of numbers and a name that looks like... Douglas?'

Em tapped a yellow line highlighting the word *mist*. 'Why is that highlighted?'

'It means my mom made some kind of annotation.' Rémy turned to the pocket at the back of the journal and took out a handwritten note. *WNG16324*.

'It's a catalogue number,' said Vaughn.

He used his phone to access the internet and an image of a painting came onto the screen. It took a few minutes to download since they were underground.

Jacob Lawrence's *The Visitors* gazed at them.

'We need to return to this painting,' Rémy said. 'Could it be any more obvious?'

'I don't think anyone should go anywhere except back to the safe-house in Glasgow,' said Vaughn, rousing from the bunk and looking worried. 'If Luca has already given the lyre to the Camarilla, Rémy's too vulnerable out in the open.'

'No,' said Rémy, his voice full of determination. 'If I can't go to Rome, then I need to follow this trail. I have to see where it leads.'

Alessandro rested a hand on Rémy's shoulder. 'I took an oath a long time ago to protect you, Rémy. Let me come with you.'

Rémy shook his head. 'Not this time,' he said. 'This is my story to see through to the end.'

'I'll go with him,' said Em. 'No offense, Professor, but a Conjuror and an Animare are stronger than a Guardian and a Conjuror. Besides, I know the family in Lawrence's painting.'

SUNDAY

AMERICA

59.

THE MOTHER WE SHARE

Jacob Lawrence's *The Visitors* was back in the permanent collection in Dallas. Em and Rémy were forced to take an awkward route to reach it, fading from a painting at the National Gallery to one in Washington and from there to the Texas city. They clumsily dropped into the Lawrence painting, with Rémy landing on top of Em.

The people in the foreground leapt to their feet with a shriek, bringing the others from the kitchen into the main room. There was a pause as they stared at Rémy. Several pairs of eyes widened, and one or two members of the family bowed low. Their respect rolled across Rémy's mind like an opening of a concerto in a dramatic wave of timpani and brass.

'Please,' he said, embarrassed. 'I'm just a kid from Chicago.'

One of the men smiled. 'You are from royal blood. Come. Ambuya has been waiting a long time to meet you.'

A child took Rémy's hand and led him into the

bedroom, where a minister sat at the side of the bed. The minister was faceless, dollops of white paint instead of any identifiable features. Em stood quietly at the bedroom door with the others, none of whom seemed able to take their eyes off Rémy.

The old woman in the bed pulled herself up against her plump pillows and patted her hair. Then she reached out her hand. Rémy took it. She pulled him closer, bringing him to sit on the edge of the bed next to her.

''Bout time you got here, my son,' she said. 'I knew your mom. My heart breaks for your loss.' Remy nodded. Ambuya went on. 'Lots of folks been talkin' about what you've been doing, and how you're gonna stop the devil once and for all.'

'I'm trying, ma'am,' said Rémy, the melody in his head a soft swish like a brush on drums. 'But the plan has changed, and I need to understand a phrase. *Musica vivificat mortuos*: music brings life to the dead. Do you know it?'

Ambuya nodded. 'It's part of Nuru's prophecy. Her story's told still among our people in Africa. She was an African queen, enslaved in Ancient Rome. Indispensable to the first king of the city, Quirinus, she was a great healer, an alchemist, the first Conjuror, some said.'

Rémy rubbed his hands on his head, thinking, processing, trying to make the same leaps that his mother even in her madness must have made. All that research she had done in the Dupree Plantation archives.

'There's something hidden in that lost slave ship,' he said at last. 'Isn't there?'

Ambuya gave a sorrowful smile. 'Something powerful enough to stop the devil.' She pulled herself up and reached for the mirror on her nightstand. 'See for yourself.'

60.

NURU'S STORY

The green-framed mirror's edges were bevelled and the glass was cloudy, but as soon as Rémy looked at its milky surface, his Conjuror's mark shot a frizz of electricity across his scalp and a swirling darkness drew Rémy inside.

He smelled sweat and shit and sorrow. He struggled to move but couldn't. Then his gut twisted. He was inside a gilded cage held aloft by a wooden pulley over a pool of water so blue it looked like glass. He thought he could see stars twinkling in its depths. His hands were shackled to the bars but his feet were hanging over the edge of the cage, almost touching the water. It was him, but not him.

The mirror's darkness danced on the edge of his vision.

The pool itself was at the centre of an open-air structure, a primitive stadium that looked like a bowl dropped into the middle of a marshy field. A frenzied chorus of cheers erupted from a crowd waving palm fronds and laurel branches. Rémy felt a thrill of accomplishment. He'd travelled in time without Matt's help after all. This was Ancient Rome.

The sun was high and the sky was clearer than he'd ever seen. No planes. No pollution. He blinked sweat from his eyes.

A legion of Roman soldiers was marching up over a hill and across the trampled field towards the stadium. Behind them stood the Roman Forum in its glory, a winding fortress wall enveloping the rolling vista that was the seven hills of Rome, the marble plinths and columns of temples and palaces on the Capitoline and Quirinal hills shining in the brilliant sunlight.

Two women in *stolas*, their skin shimmering like copper in the sun's rays were flanking him, one holding a lyre... *the lyre*... and the other holding a set of ivory pipes in her long fingers. Three bronze cauldrons bubbling with silver liquid were balanced on the edge of the pool.

The frieze. Had to be.

Or at least, the moment which the frieze depicted.

The woman with the pitch pipes reminded Rémy of Minerva, the goddess he had met when Luca had trapped him inside *The Flaying of Marsyas* in the Tomb of the Martyrs under the Tiber. He studied the woman with the lyre, her dark hair long, a spray of freckles across her sharp nose and high cheekbones. As the soldiers marched closer, Rémy recognized the uniform of the Camarilla, and their commander. Luca Ferrante, vast and muscular, led the column.

Then time skipped. The crowd's cheers were deafening now, the drums in Rémy's head crashing symbols.

An African woman, Nuru, walked in front of Luca beneath a canopy of laurel branches. Her head had been shaved, but she held it high. Behind Luca, an Emperor rode on a she-wolf as big as an elephant, his body gnarled with age, his skin yellow and paper thin.

'*Ecce unus est!*' The crowd chanted, and Rémy finally understood.

Behold the one!

But was it Nuru they were referring to?

Luca's wings were folded against his centurion's leather vest, the tip of his sword touching the curve of Nuru's back, prodding her forward. Every hand in the first ring of seats was reaching out, desperate to touch Nuru as she glided past.

The great she-wolf lay down beside the pool, and one of the women helped the Emperor down beside the gilded cage. Rémy could smell the anticipation seeping through his skin.

Time skipped again. The she-wolf snarled. Nuru now held the lyre. She shook her head and Luca laughed. Rémy felt the air thin and saw Luca's wings expand. He could feel the boy in the cage begin to suffocate.

'Stop! Let him live,' said Nuru, her eyes wide in anger. 'I will conjure for you.'

'Bring forth my kingdom and you both may live,' said the old Emperor.

Nuru's fingers picked an eerie discordant melody on the lyre. The notes came slowly at first, then faster, sending the sound out in golden ribbons that coiled above the pool. The pool bubbled into liquid gold as the music spread.

Time skipped. Rémy felt as if he had dropped a thousand feet on a carnival ride. Nuru's bloody fingers were still plucking the lyre, but the sky was no longer clear blue. It was alive, crowded with flailing limbs and howling heads, misshapen bodies and contorted torsos. The stone seats of the stadium were packed with hundreds of souls in agony. Their screams, their torment, was sucking the life from him.

Then Rémy smelled oranges.

The mirror's darkness began to creep inward, clouding the edges of the grotesque scene. Rémy fought the sensation. He had to stay. He had to see what happened.

Swarms of beetles surged from the pool, the water thick and viscous.

The mirror's darkness edged closer.

Not yet!

Nuru's playing reached a crescendo. The thick golden liquid was suddenly animated, transforming into a leafless barren tree. A beastly figure, part faun, part man, began to emerge from the centre of the tree's pocked, splintered golden trunk.

Nuru nodded at the boy in the cage – at Rémy. A set of pipes had appeared in the boy's hand. He put them to his lips, and a melody soared free above the field in a million silver daggers of light.

The cage sprang open. The boy leapt on to the altar stone as it cleaved in two, half of it crashing into the thick pool. The tormented souls reached for him, their arms grasping, grabbing. Nuru kept playing. The boy kept playing. The tree of life began to slow and stiffen, the beast freezing in place.

The mirror's darkness was almost upon him.

Time shifted.

61.

ANNIE'S LAMENT

Rémy had read the passage in his mother's diary too many times not to know what was coming.

He was in a tight space, his breathing shallow and constricted as if someone was sitting on his chest. His hands were those of a child, thin wrists in iron manacles, feet unbound. The child was tucked into a narrow wooden space, she shoved a package wrapped in oilskin into a hollow then she peered between wooden slats damp with brine.

The air was stagnant, the reek of decaying flesh and rancid food clinging to the slats of wood. Buzzing flies carpeted the deck and swarmed over the limp sails, while rows of glistening black ravens sat like judges on the main masts.

Through the slats, Rémy saw the butchered body of a young man. Fat bluebottle flies covered his head and his mouth and what remained of his genitals. A bloody machete stood impaled in the splintered planks of the

242

deck. Rémy's gorge rose. Castration was a punishment for disobedience on a slave ship, a message meant to strip any vestige of pride or power that remained. Rémy wished the child would turn away, but she didn't; wouldn't.

He caught a glimpse of a tall graceful man wearing a ruffled shirt, an embroidered tunic, blue pantaloons and silver buckled shoes, wiping blood from his hands with his handkerchief. The ship's captain hung from the main mast overhead, his face engorged, his body swaying with the ship's steady rocking. The child – Rémy – dropped her eyes to a young woman squatting on the deck over her newborn infant. The woman's thin body was covered in a caul of sweat.

Don Grigori, the monster who'd murdered his mom, leisurely tugged the machete free, leaned over and sliced through the newborn's umbilical cord. The woman pulled her infant protectively against her bloody tunic as Don Grigori leaned over and spoke to her in a high-pitched voice.

'*Musica vivicat mortuos…*'

Cradling her infant in her arms, the young mother glanced towards the child's hiding space. The mother was the double of Rémy's mom.

The anguish of the moment crushed Rémy. He understood now that his mother's journal entries were more than just clues to him about his future. They were a testament to their past, her book of lamentations. This was his family, slaughtered and grieving, frightened and alone. He had read his mother's words so many times but they had been just that. Words. He'd never felt this level of rage or such an epiphany before.

A thunderous crack tore through the trees and a figure dropped on to the upper deck, swords drawn, a yellow turban tied around his head, two straps crossing on his chest holding his daggers.

Rémy wanted to cheer.

'You're too late, Moor,' said Don Grigori warily. 'I will take this infant when I have finished with the mother, and you will not stop me. My master has need of him.'

The ship rocked violently in the water, angry waves crashing onto the deck as Alessandro lunged. With the full force of his momentum, he stabbed his dagger into a large packing crate that stood on the deck, aiming for the Inquisitor's portrait that Rémy knew must be packed inside, allowing the Inquisitor and Don Grigori to escape Europe.

Don Grigori dropped the machete and howled like a banshee. His skin lit up in a flash of white light, then dulled to a powdery translucence. A grey, amorphous creature surrounded by swarms of flies was sucked away, through the broken planks of the crate. Into the damaged painting, Rémy guessed, to recover as best he could.

Crouching at the mutilated torso of the man on the deck, Alessandro said a quiet prayer as he lifted a familiar golden talisman from around the dead man's neck and draped it carefully around the young mother's throat.

'I am forever at your service,' Rémy heard him say.

Rémy's hand instinctively went to his own neck, to feel the same talisman hanging where it always did. But he only felt the child's bare trembling skin. The talisman was not his, yet.

Alessandro glanced through the slats at Rémy. 'Come, child,' he said simply as he prepared to destroy what was left of the crate. 'You're safe now.'

Suddenly a riot of voices and whistles could be heard from the shoreline. Musket fire popped, and a hail of musket balls ripped into the deck. Cursing, Alessandro leapt to the railing and dived head first into the Mississippi. The crate remained where it was.

And that's when the child began to sing. Silver ribbons of music flirted with the breeze, dancing over the dark green water, dipping and swirling above Rémy's head, snaking through the trees towards the plantation house beyond the sugar cane fields.

Rémy felt himself detach from the child's body. In the distance, he could make out the pillars of the wrap-around porch and the palm-frond blades of the fans spinning silently in the warm night breeze. Men and women were drinking on the wide veranda. All around him, the bayou was thick with lush green foliage, glossy plants with white flowers shaped like trumpets and live oaks knee deep in the bayou, their branches adorned with kudzu. Willow branches skirted the surface of the water like the hem of a ball gown. A great blue heron lifted off and swept over the bayou. Eucalyptus, honeysuckle, jasmine and the sharp metallic stench of blood hung in the air.

The music stopped.

LOUISIANA

62.

WADE IN THE WATER

Rémy sat on the bow of a ramshackle barge, a square wooden wheelhouse and cabin in the centre of its deck, the pea-soup water of the Mississippi lapping against its hollow hull. His bare feet were dangling over the edge, his toes flicking its buggy surface. Behind him Em was in a black neoprene dive suit, the pale skin on her neck covered in a thin sheen of sweat and a thick layer of mosquitoes.

The *Quirinus* had sunk somewhere in this delta. It was after midnight, yet the temperature was still in the thirties and the humidity was like a wet sponge on his skin. Every few seconds he heard Em slap a mosquito. Strangely, they were not biting Rémy. It was as if he had a protective shield over his body. He watched them swarming above his skin, then buzzing away.

'I can't believe you don't have one frickin' bite,' Em grumbled, pulling the zipper up under her chin and waving at a cloud of insects in the air above her head.

She finished checking their diving equipment while Rémy checked the journal for further details.

'Quirinus was the first king of Rome,' Rémy offered after a moment. 'His body was taken by the First Watcher. I saw it all in the mirror.'

'I thought the first king was Romulus?'

'Same man. Quirinus was a Sabine warrior, believed to be the deified Romulus.'

Rémy dropped his mom's journal into a diver's bag, sealing it before he stuck it inside a pocket on his wetsuit.

'Why has no one salvaged this ship before?' Em wanted to know.

'No one knows it's here,' said Rémy, zipping up his dive suit. 'And the devil probably guards it.'

'That's not funny.' Em dragged over Rémy's gear and checked his air flow and numbers. 'Remind me again why I'm doing all these checks alone?'

'Because you're the more experienced diver.'

Rémy used his binoculars and zoomed in on the pitched roof of the Dupree Plantation house visible above the tree-line. Seeing nothing else of note, he was about to drop the binoculars into the front pocket of his backpack when a flash of light on the horizon caught his eyes.

'Did you see that?'

Em looked up from testing her breathing tube and glanced in the direction of open water. Heat lightning strafed across the sky for a second, creating a pillow of blue and pink between the sea and the sky. 'What, that?'

'No.' He put the binoculars to his eyes again, slowly scanning the horizon. One or two shrimpers bobbed across his line of sight off to the west, but nothing else.

'Quit worrying,' Em advised. 'We're on our own.'

She spat into her mouthpiece and rubbed her spit into the tube with her fingers before fitting her mask. She gave Rémy a thumbs-up and a smile.

Rémy forced a smile in return.

63.

SORROW SONGS

Moonlight drizzled through the cypress and willows crouching on the bank. Pines and live oaks rustled in the light breeze that brought no relief from the heat, even though the sun had set hours ago. The twisted grey branches of dogwood trees looked like arms delving into the stagnant pools of the delta.

In her animated wetsuit, Em climbed off the deck and slid into the murky shallows.

'How deep do you think we'll need to go?' she asked, bobbing in the water.

'We have fifty metres of rope, but I don't think we'll need more than fifteen,' said Rémy. 'Twenty at the most. This bayou isn't as deep as some of the others in this region.'

He lifted the heavy rusted iron anchor and dropped it over the side of the barge, waiting until he felt the tightening tug on the guide rope. Then he wrapped and knotted the rope on an iron link on the side of the barge.

He adjusted his mask and tapped his gauge, slowly sliding into the water next to Em.

The radio clicked in his ear, her voice clear. 'You good?'

'Fine,' said Rémy, watching Em's glimmering silhouette dive down in front of him.

'It's scary dark down here.'

Rémy was still treading water at the surface. He ducked down. 'We could be right above Atlantis and not know it.'

Using the anchor line as her guide, Em pointed the beam of her torch in front of her. Rémy stayed as close to her feet as he could. Her body glowed like Nemo in the murky water.

When they reached the anchor, Em scanned the area, the torch illuminating only a few metres in front of them.

'I can't see anything that looks like a wreck,' said Em in Rémy's earpiece. 'Maybe we got the coordinates wrong.'

'No,' said Rémy firmly. 'This is the place.'

He scanned his torch in the other direction. Thoughtfully, he picked up the anchor and dropped it again, sending a cloud of sediment, eels, and water snakes swirling around them.

'Stop it,' Em warned, batting away the snakes. 'You'll draw alligators.'

But Rémy kept lifting and dropping the anchor. On his third try, it disappeared. Crouching down, he pointed the beam of his torch through a hole at his feet.

'We couldn't see it because we're standing on it,' he said in triumph. 'Em, the anchor landed on what's left of the deck.'

Em leaned into the hole, the dangling anchor next to her head. Rémy heard a long slow moan in his ears as she jerked back violently. Even in the gloom, he could see terror in her eyes.

'I can't go in there,' she stammered. 'It's too awful. The emotions... Rémy, I can feel them like a million needles behind my eyes. And taste them... the iron, the blood...'

Rémy's adrenaline was surging through his body. He leaned cautiously into the ragged hole, one arm linked on the anchor rope. He let his breath out in short rapid bursts. The hull was full of skeletons manacled to each other, hands to the feet of the person in front of them, tethered to their floating coffin.

64.

MISSISSIPPI RIVER BLUES

Rémy swam slowly above the bones of his ancestors. Don Grigori had killed them all, it seemed – not just the Conjuror. He took his time, moving from one side of the hull towards the other, his flashlight running across the crevices and the cracks of the ship. The mournful drone that had accompanied him since the Professor's underground lair was becoming a weeping of voices, the same bluesy requiem he'd heard inside the Lawrence painting.

At the bow of the ship, his heart sank. A hole as big as a truck was open to the murky black water. If anything had been hidden, it had floated away or been salvaged centuries ago.

'Bones,' he managed to tell Em, returning to her side. 'From stern to bow. And a big fucking hole.' The chorus of voices in his head was softer again, a quiet drone of sound. 'But there's something down here. I can hear it.'

'And I can feel it.'

The oxygen in Rémy's tank was lower than expected, with around a third left. He'd been breathing too heavily. 'We're running out of time,' he said, tapping at his oxygen gauge. 'Let's do a sweep of the area.'

Em took his hand, kicking towards the bow. They both held their torches out in front, to widen their field of vision. The sounds inside Rémy's head grew louder and his Conjuror's mark stabbed his neck as they swam along the top of the broken hull. When they got closer to the bow, the howls changed to weeping again, cascading over him like ice water.

A huge figure lurched up in front of them. Em shrieked and dropped her torch. It bounced off the bottom of the hull and lodged in the silt beneath the wreck, its beam flickering as it sank into the murky bottom of the delta and was gone.

Em tightened her grip on Rémy's hand. 'What the hell is that?'

The chorus in Rémy's head was screaming. They were on top of what they were searching for. He knew it. Picturing the little oilcloth package the child had been holding on board the ship, he levelled his torch.

'It's the figurehead,' he said.

The great wooden face was cracked in half. What was left of it looked like it was charred, thick black tar covering its entire surface.

'Pan,' said Em, taking a closer look. 'The god of music.'

'When Nuru opened Chaos with the lyre – before the young Conjuror shut it again – Pan was guarding the tree of life,' Rémy said, thinking. He'd told Em about the awful visions he had experienced. 'And when Zach and his mom helped me in Luca's underground lair, I saw the petrified version of the tree and of Pan. I think the mirror was showing me a way to stop the Camarilla, and it's hidden right here. Inside this figurehead. Inside Pan.

'It's literally screaming at me to be found.'

65.

LAVENDER AND GRASS

Callum came round with a bang, a thunderous headache playing bass drum behind his eyes. He felt sick. The Roman Empire was going to rise again, thanks to some serious supernatural shit. Christ, his head hurt.

He was fully clothed, and on a bed big enough for a family of four in a room straight out of a Dickens novel. He moved his hands and feet, relieved he wasn't tied up. Someone had taken his shoes. When he sat up, the drum got louder.

The room was dark, floor to ceiling curtains on tall windows, but he could see the dim light of day breaking through. The walls were papered in a velvet flock design and covered in portraits of scowling old men in military uniforms, one or two on thrones, women in high ruffled dresses with children or dogs on their laps, and a row of horse paintings, many more appealing to look at than the people. It was the kind of art tracing a family of wealth and privilege over centuries. A whiff of lavender and grass tugged his senses and he rolled to a sitting position, feeling fresh air ruffling the curtains.

Someone had set two bottles of water, an empty glass, and a packet of Alka Seltzer on a side table. He opened one of the bottles for the fizz, ignoring the glass and dropping the tablets directly into the bottle. What he really needed was an Irn-Bru and an explanation.

His watch said 3:25pm. Given that he had confronted Fiera Orsini around 2am in the centre of Trastevere, he'd just had the best sleep since Pietra had died.

His gut twisted with grief. With his hands on his hips and his head bowed, he swallowed until the nausea passed and the constellation of floaters vanished from his peripheral vision.

Slugging the rest of the water, he dug around in the bedside tables, where he found a letter opener, blank stationery and a pair of wool socks.

He slipped the letter opener under the waistband of his jeans and crept barefoot out the door, into a plaid carpeted hallway with two more bedrooms on either side of a staircase. The place was tall and narrow, a townhouse in a city somewhere. He could hear traffic noises outside, a horn honking and a screech of a lorry or a bus's airbrakes. The house itself was quiet, apart from a radio playing classical music somewhere downstairs, and yet it felt as if it were breathing. When Callum looked downstairs, he thought he saw the foyer walls expand

and contract for a split second. But then he blinked and everything looked normal.

He returned to the bedroom and closed the door quietly behind him. At the tall window, he pulled open the heavy curtains and looked outside.

'Oh shit. *London*?'

LOUISIANA

66.

GATOR AID

Em tied the anchor end of the rope around the upper part of the figurehead, knotting it the way Zach had taught her when she was learning to sail. Then she gathered up the rest of the rope and kicked to the surface. Rémy helped her back on to the deck of the barge, and together they tied the rope to the rusty winch. Rémy prepared to crank the wheel and raise the figurehead to the surface.

A piercing shot came out of nowhere, hitting one of the oxygen tanks. The tank exploded.

The blast threw Em back into the water. A series of shots hit the barge, sending flames shooting into the sky. Pieces of the burning wheelhouse dropped like Molotov cocktails into the water. As fast as he could, Rémy uncoiled the winch, grabbed the loose end of the rope and jumped into the flaming water.

'Em!' he shouted. 'Where are you?'

Another volley of shots skimmed the barge and ricocheted into the second oxygen tank. The tank rocketed away over the water screaming like a missile, exploding into a copse of trees on the other side of the bayou.

'Em! EM!'

Up at the shoreline, Rémy saw two 'gators slip one after the other into the water. He kicked harder, dragging the rope with him. When it caught on something, it took him three tugs to free it.

He felt something grazing his leg. He whipped round, expecting to punch a 'gator.

'Put this on,' Em urged, handing him a mask. 'It was floating in the water. I still had mine.' She glanced around. 'Vaughn was right. The Camarilla are everywhere.'

'We need to get out of the water,' said Rémy, doggy-paddling desperately while trying to tie the rope attached to the figurehead around his waist.

Em beckoned. 'Give it to me. I'm a stronger swimmer.'

The 'gators were nosing past the debris, heading their way. Rémy didn't argue. He knotted the rope around Em's waist. Em kicked into freestyle, moving sluggishly but still moving forward.

Smoke billowed over the tree-line on both sides of the bayou, sealing the area like a lid. A volley of shots hit the water, this time far too close to Rémy's head. He went under, heading in Em's direction, following the figurehead.

When he came up for air, he crashed into a tree limb stretched across the water like a scolding finger, tearing the skin above his right eye. Swearing loudly, he struggled to free himself from the tangle of its roots. He wasn't as fast a swimmer as Em, especially without his fins, but he wasn't going to drown. He flipped under again and followed the glow of her wetsuit deeper towards the other side of the bayou, doing his best to forget about the 'gators behind them. His Tia Rosa had filled his head with stories about the spirits of the river and how the 'gators protected those that lived near and on it. She'd told him 'gators never ate black men. Rémy was pretty sure he didn't want to be the first to test the theory.

Suddenly he couldn't see Em any more. He raised his head above the water. A series of shots went whizzing past his head and he ducked again.

'Em!'

'Over here. The rope's stuck.'

Rémy helped her, but the dead weight wouldn't budge. The rope was caught in a tangle of tree roots.

'The figurehead is stuck. I can't pull it any further. And the alligators are coming.'

'Leave it,' Rémy said. 'Get on to the shore. I've got this.'

Em scrambled out of the water, rolling behind a thick copse of the trees hanging like loose teeth over the edge of the bayou. 'They smell food,' she warned Rémy as he splashed back into the murk.

Wading out until he felt his knees scrape on the tree roots snagging the rope and the figurehead, Rémy stood up, knee deep in the water. Only then did he look back.

One of the 'gators was just a few metres away. Rémy whistled, a long high pitched note. The 'gator kept coming. Rémy raised the pitch. The melody became a spiral of mist that spread from him across the water, settling like dry ice around the 'gators. The water crackled and popped and turned to ice, freezing the 'gators in place like popsicles.

More shots whizzed into the trees overhead. It was hopeless. Rémy backed away from the snagged rope, waded ashore and grabbed Em's hand. They crashed through the thick brush to the cover of an enormous live oak, kudzo coiling around its branches like streamers.

The mosquitoes on this side of the river were swarming in full attack mode. Although Em's neoprene suit was zipped all the way to her chin, her hands and feet were already a landscape of fiery red welts.

'You're getting eaten alive,' said Rémy. 'We can't stay exposed like this.'

Another shot peeled past his ear. He threw himself on top of Em, but not before the bullet had torn across her thigh and slammed into the tree behind them.

'Aargh!'

Em grabbed her leg, blood seeping through her fingers, her face grey with pain.

'I don't understand,' said Rémy in frustration. 'How can they see us? The smoke and trees should be shielding us.'

'They can hear us,' gasped Em. 'You have to stop conjuring.'

Rémy glanced over his shoulder. 'We need to move. Can you put weight on your leg?'

Em nodded, wincing. 'Do you have anything else to defend us with? Your knife?'

'Lost it in the explosion along with our backpacks. Thank God I put the journal in my wetsuit pocket.'

They pushed their way deeper into the everglades. When they had enough cover from the shoreline, Rémy helped Em to sit on a felled tree. Something skittered from a pool beneath the trunk and into a nearby marsh. A woodpecker tapped above their heads. Ribbons of gold light washed over the bayou.

'Find me a stick or a rock, something to draw with,' Em said through clenched teeth. 'I need to animate before the sun sets, or whoever's shooting at us will see the animation glow and we'll be sitting ducks.'

67.

A SONG IN THE NIGHT

Rémy rubbed his hand over his stubbled hair, trying to think. He'd stopped shaving his head, saving the effort for when he had regular access to soap and water and showers again. The rasp of bristles helped him to focus.

Everything on the ground was wet or muddy. Looking up, Rémy wrenched at a couple of branches overhead and handed them to Em, who selected the sharpest and dug it into the mud. She animated a roll of bandage first that Rémy wrapped tightly around her leg. Then she tackled protective clothing, with hats and gloves that made them both look like beekeepers. Finally, she created food and water. Rémy tried and failed to contain his disappointment at the ham and cheese sandwiches and the bottled water.

Em's face was still contorted with pain. 'Best I could do in the circumstances. Need my energy for bigger things.'

Next was a dark green boat with a small motor. The glow from the animations blended with the sun rising over the bayou, and no one else shot at them as they ate. The blood was clotting on Em's leg. It wasn't much more than a graze.

'Do you think they're gone?' Em said, wiping her mouth.

'No.' Rémy emptied his bottle of water in one gulp. 'I think they're waiting for our next move.'

'What's on the other side of this bayou?'

'More bayou.'

As the sun rose, Em animated a winch to pull the rope free from the tree roots and haul the figurehead ashore. Rémy rolled it on to its back. The ram stared up at them. Thick algae and muck wept from its eyes and a wide crack around its mouth gave it a malevolent grin. When this had been on the front of the ship, it would have been painted a brilliant white, with eyes of onyx. Rémy rubbed the curve of one of the horns, revealing a flash of gold.

'Creepy,' said Em with a shudder.

'I have to conjure,' Rémy said. 'Sorry.'

Em glanced around. 'Try and keep it quiet,' she advised.

Rémy began to hum quietly. After a moment, he snatched a handsaw from mid-air and sawed both the horns off. The ram's head looked even more malevolent.

Each horn was as wide as Rémy's upper arms. Rémy

tapped the curl of the horn, at the point where the golden metal was the thickest. 'In here.'

Voices carried from the water. They heard a small outboard motor start up.

'They're getting closer,' said Em, tense again. 'We could take the boat I animated earlier, it's just back there. Give me the horns.'

The mark at the back of Rémy's neck itched seductively as he sawed at the horns. He handed them to Em for safekeeping.

She got up from the log with some difficulty. It was clear that her leg was still hurting. 'Time to get the hell out of here.'

Rémy glanced towards the water. 'They'll follow the boat. We need to shake them off.'

Em paused. 'What are you going to do?'

'Scare the shit out of them.'

*

Rémy sprinted back into the trees. Em closed her eyes for a second. A wind rustled the branches above her head. The scent of oranges tickled her nose.

'That was fast,' she said, looking up.

LONDON

68.

WATCHING AIRPLANES

Zach Butler was staring out of the Orangery window at Kensington Palace and the Round Pond. It was late afternoon and tourists, university students, and gaggles of school children filled the pedestrian avenue that criss-crossed Kensington Gardens. He was working on a laptop of his own invention, monitoring Luca Ferrante in a 3D hologram map hovering from the screen.

Zach spotted his mother coming out of the trees in the park. He watched her dodge around a family trying to negotiate tourists on Segways and jog towards him. He wondered how his childhood might have been different if Orianna had returned to his life sooner. He understood now why she had stayed away, but understanding hadn't come with acceptance. At least not yet. He could only cope with one abandonment at a time, and Em's was still pretty raw.

'What's Luca doing now?' asked Orianna, breezing into the Orangery.

'Terminal Five at Heathrow.' Zach pointed to the twinkling image on the 3D hologram.

'Have I told you recently how truly brilliant you are?' Orianna was looking closely at the hologram. 'A twenty-first century da Vinci.'

He smiled at the compliment. 'I've got no idea what he's doing, but he's not moved from that spot at Heathrow for a couple of hours now. I'm worried he won't hold up the bargain he's made with us for the lyre.'

'He will,' said Orianna. There was a curious confidence in the way she said it. 'But he needs to stay on Cecilia's plan until the very end.'

'How can you be so sure he'll help us when we need him?'

'His human nature was always stronger than his divine one. I mean, look at what he's been doing for hours.' She laughed. 'Sitting at the airport, watching planes.'

'Are you worried that time has changed his feelings?'

She cupped Zach's face in her hands and looked into his eyes. 'Of course I'm worried. I'm terrified. But I've waited a long time for this all to end and we're prepared.'

'I never feel anything but calm from you,' signed Zach. Orianna's emotional temperature never modulated enough to trigger Zach's Guardian senses, even when she had every right to be freaking out.

'I wouldn't have survived in the Camarilla all this time if they could sense my emotions. I learned a long time ago how to put up... what would you call it? A psychic firewall?'

She was about to squeeze his hand, but he pulled away. She let her hands drop to her lap. 'It would be foolish of us not to be concerned. We're working against our hearts. But Luca has the lyre and we're trusting that he won't hand it over. Orion has the Sacred Chord safely hidden in Scotland. According to your last meeting with Vaughn, the Conjuror is safe too. And of course, the Inquisitor is still bound in his painting in the Vatican's secret vault.'

'That's what's worrying me,' signed Zach. 'If Cecilia is planning to open Chaos and raise the Watchers during tonight's concert in Rome, then she needs everything in place. Right?'

Orianna nodded.

'So she either believes she's going to get everything together in time, or she has something else planned.'

Something flashed across Orianna's face. Zach tasted pineapple and vinegar and for the first time ever felt a soupçon of fear from his mother.

'Perhaps we need to alert Vaughn,' Orianna said. 'Just in case I'm wrong about the First Watcher still being bound in his portrait.'

'We can't risk another meeting,' Zach pointed out. 'Especially after what Cecilia did to Victor.'

Orianna sighed. 'We also don't really have time for another meeting. Cecilia expects us at the Vatican's private salon in four hours, and we still have to get to Rome. All we can do is warn Vaughn online.'

Zach swiped fast to another hologram and sent an encrypted message to Vaughn.

First Watcher may be unbound.

He looked back out the window, and focused his attention on the family on the Segways. They'd made it to the entrance of Kensington Palace, but were just realizing that it was closing for the day. Even from this distance, their disappointment tasted like rancid butter.

His phone vibrated.

'That was fast,' said Orianna in surprise.

Zach pushed his blond hair from his face and stared at the screen. 'It's Matt. Again.'

Orianna sighed. 'Tell him to meet us in Rome in three hours. We may need all the help we can get.'

Zach sent the email, wondering how Matt would respond. They hadn't spoken in months. He glanced down at Luca on the hologram.

'Shit,' he said in alarm.

The hologram flickered for a second. Zach wiped his suddenly sweaty palms on his jeans and keyed in a string of code that ran across the hologram in a mash-up of Latin, Greek and Asci. Instantly, a paragraph of similar code fluttered in the centre of the screen, as if an imaginary source of air was blowing on it from inside. Orianna stood behind Zach and they watched the lambent line of code move around like quicksilver.

'What's he done?' Orianna said sharply.

'I don't know,' Zach signed after a moment. 'But air traffic is being diverted to Dublin and Glasgow. I think Heathrow just went into lockdown.' He checked another screen and frowned. 'Callum's on the move too.'

'Find him,' Orianna ordered.

69.

FROM A WINDOW

A couple of hours earlier, Callum had dropped from his second window in as many days, sprinting across a manicured garden and through a gate with the names *Violet and Anthea Kitten* on a brass plate. He raced down Raphael Terrace until he saw a familiar Underground sign and headed in that direction.

Outside Earl's Court tube station, Callum looked in his wallet. He had no cash, but he did have an emergency credit card his parents had given him when he left for university. He hoped they'd kept it active. At an RBS cash machine, he maxed out what he could withdraw. He knew it was risky, but he needed to get back to Rome. He would not be cut out of whatever shit was going down in the Eternal City just because he wasn't some kind of Harry Potter.

He took the Piccadilly Line directly to Terminal 5 and headed upstairs towards the archipelago of check-in counters. Since he had no luggage, he went directly to security, hoping that news of Victor Moretti's murder had stayed in Rome.

August was peak travel time for Brits to Europe. Callum tucked himself into the line behind a chatty family, and used their exuberance to lose himself while still keeping his eyes on the police and security personnel watching the slow-moving lines. When he came out the other side of the line, he headed straight to the gate.

Inside Terminal 5 Callum threaded his way through the crowd towards the great glass walls that looked out on to the gates and the runways beyond. He paused before taking the escalator down to the gate, and dropped into Waterstones to get a book for the flight. That's when he noticed a vast shadow sweeping over a nearby runway. It moved like a plane that was coming in too low and too fast to make its landing. A few travellers screamed. One or two began to run back towards security. The silhouette blocked out the sunlight as it swooped closer, drenching the gates in darkness. It was coming towards the great glass wall, and it showed no signs of stopping.

Callum felt as if he was underwater. Everything was muted and distant. The terminal lights flickered. A row of light bulbs on the roof exploded, showering sparks and glass on passengers below, who covered their heads and ran.

70.

FREEBIRD

Luca swerved before hitting the glass wall and landed on the roof of the terminal. He adjusted his position so that he faced the runway, and dropped again. His feet hit the tarmac three times before he began his transformation, his massive wings opening behind him like a black cloak stitched with silver threads of light, lifting him off the ground, his body expanding mid-air, morphing into his angelic form. Directly ahead of him, a wide-body four-engine Airbus A380 was accelerating into its take-off.

Luca laughed as the backdraft from the Airbus rushed over him in a fine mist. The plane's nose tilted and its engines roared. There was just enough space between its tail and the runway for Luca to swoop beneath it. The plane banked into a shockingly steep turn, rolling left and right before stabilizing and climbing into its original flight path.

Luca roared, the sound like thunder as he shot above

the plane into the heavens, the smell of burning fuel and hot rubber filling him, invigorating and intoxicating him.

Who had his loyalty? His father and the Camarilla? Or Sebina and Orion?

No more games. Time was running out.

LEAVING ON A JET PLANE

At Heathrow the power went out and the emergency lights kicked in. The entire terminal shook violently, knocking a decorative steel beam onto one directly beneath it, leaving both balancing precariously in the air. The space became a log jam of people, all fighting to get out. Airport workers caught outside had either rolled under luggage carts or crashed through the ground floor doors. Alarms were blaring and the lights at every gate were flashing red. A plane that had been taxiing towards a nearby gate had screeched to a stop, impaling itself on the tail of another plane.

Callum stood, transfixed by the great swooping silhouette, which was growing smaller by the minute. Whatever it was had moving wings that fluttered in the dimming light.

Two strong hands grabbed Callum's shoulders and pulled him back. Callum pivoted on his heels, lifted an elbow and jabbed at his attacker who ducked, missed the point of Callum's elbow, and used his own to stab

Callum's throat. On his knees gasping for breath, Callum looked up. It was the young man from Villa Orsini. Zach.

Callum opened his mouth, but Zach simply glared. The message was clear.

No time for talking.

He yanked Callum to his feet and rushed him through the rapidly emptying terminal. Making a sudden swerve, he pulled Callum through an unmarked door into a stairwell. The door alarm started up, fighting to make itself heard above the general cacophony.

'I'm going back to Rome,' said Callum stubbornly.

Zach shot him a look of mingled amusement and pity. *How exactly?* his gestures said. It was a problem Callum was trying not to think about.

The stairwell was empty and smelled of petrol and piss. Zach dragged him down the stairs in leaps and bounds. At the bottom of three flights of stairs, they barrelled through a door. The petrol-scented air hit Callum like a blow. They were out on the tarmac, on the far side of the terminal. The loading zone was empty, the sky lit up with the glow of emergency vehicles surrounding the airport. A handful of helicopters were strafing the scene with searchlights. Callum managed to keep on Zach's heels as they crashed through two more locked doors, setting off more alarms as they went, until they exited four gates away from where they started.

They were in a hangar with two private jets parked and empty. One of the jets was taxiing out of the open hangar doors with its own door hanging open like a loose tooth. A woman with long black hair swirling around her head was beckoning at them from the slowly moving plane. Zach reached the lowered steps first and scrambled inside without a backwards glance. Callum jumped, hitting his shins on the steps. The woman grabbed his hand, her upper body strength surprising Callum. She pulled him inside before hauling up the door and locking it. She thumped hard on the cock-pit door. The plane accelerated, bounced out on to the nearby runway and took off.

Breathless, Callum scrambled up from the floor of the tiny galley. 'Are we going back to Rome?' he demanded.

No one answered. Callum shot a look at Zach, who had already buckled himself into a cream leather seat. Zach grinned back, unperturbed. Slowly, Callum took a seat as far away from Zach as possible, clicked his seatbelt and closed his eyes.

The plane was almost vertical as it rose into the evening sky. After a few minutes it levelled out. Callum glanced around. The cabin had seating for six in swivelling reclining seats, a flat screen TV and a private bathroom at the rear. Everything was accessorized with mahogany and silver accents, including the woman staring at him. Her skin was brown, sweat beading across her sharp cheekbones, a cuff of silver bracelets half-covering a tattoo on the inside of her wrist. She was about his mum's age, Callum guessed, and she was pissed off.

The woman leaned forward and put her hands on his

knees, squeezing her fingers under his kneecaps. Callum flinched from the pain that shot up to his groin. She released the pressure briefly.

'You shouldn't have run,' she said.

Callum felt like his brain was running two minutes behind his body. He turned to Zach, leaning over his laptop watching some kind of hologram weather map with a storm front moving quickly across it. Zach didn't look up, so Callum turned back.

'Who are you?'

'Orianna.'

The woman let go of his legs and sat back. The plane lurched in turbulence and Callum gripped the armrests as the jet steadied itself.

'What the hell was that?' he said. 'Back at the airport? It had wings.'

'*That* was the reason we needed you to stay hidden in Raphael Terrace.'

Callum's brain was a waterfall of questions. 'You both work for Signora Orsini?'

Orianna poured two fingers of whisky from a crystal decanter. She handed one to Callum, who shot the liquid and refused another, taking up a bottle of water instead. Zach hadn't lifted his head from the storm front he appeared to be tracking on his screen.

Orianna sipped the whisky, a disconcerting smile on her face. 'You got yourself involved in a world of crazy, didn't you?' she said presently.

'What happened back at the airport?' Callum repeated.

'A Nephilim happened. A creature, half-human, half-angel, named Lucius Ferrante. Likes to call himself Luca.'

Callum thought about what Signora Orsini had told him, about angels and portals to Chaos. This was a world of crazy for sure. 'I'm thinking he's not on our side?'

Orianna sighed. 'Luca's on his own side, and that makes him as dangerous as the men and women he purports to serve.'

'The Camarilla?'

She looked a little more approving. 'Glad you've been paying attention.'

The plane banked into a steep turn before correcting itself. Callum spilled his water. He glimpsed a series of rapid hand movements from Zach. Orianna's face paled.

'What did Zach say?' said Callum, his gut clenching. He was afraid of the answer.

'Luca has noticed that we are following him.'

'Why the hell are we following an angel?' shouted Callum.

'A Nephilim,' said Orianna, her eyes back on Callum. 'There's a difference.'

Zach was intent on his laptop again, a faint flickering glow rising from its screen. The plane rocked violently, popping open the overhead bins. Callum looked anxiously out at the sky aglow in pink and orange.

A great emerald eye appeared in the porthole window. Orianna ducked as Callum reared back. The plane flipped into a roll, sending anything not fastened down flying around the cabin. Callum slammed back, then forward. He ducked seconds before the decanter flew against the headrest of his seat. He glimpsed an impossibly vast black and silver wing.

'He's playing with us,' said Orianna.

'Can't you cast a spell, or draw, or whatever you do and get us out of here?'

'I am not a witch.' Orianna seemed amused. 'Besides, what would you have me draw?'

'Parachutes?'

Zach looked ghostly, his body wraithlike and surrounded in the glow of his computer screen. The plane creaked loudly, dipped again. Callum bit his tongue. Tasted blood. Outside the window the sunset was a screaming orange.

Suddenly the plane pitched again. This time it didn't pull up. Through the fear and nausea, Callum glimpsed Zach. He was completely engulfed in the light from his computer, man and machine as one.

72.

WIND BENEATH MY WINGS

To get through the gut-wrenching terror of the plunging plane, Callum summoned an image of Pietra smiling at him, a pencil stuck behind her ear, her reading glasses perched on the tip of her nose, a mug of coffee raised at her lips. Grief swelled through his panic. He let his tears flow.

The plane was in a steep dive. The engines were squealing. And then – they were not. Everything shook for a minute or two before the plane levelled out. Callum inhaled deeply and opened his eyes, his nail marks visible on the leather arm rest.

Zach was trembling, teeth chattering, fingers limp on his computer. Both he and his machine were covered in a sheen of pixels as if someone had dropped a glitter bomb on them.

'What happened?' croaked Callum. 'How—'

'Zach became the plane and out-manoeuvred Luca.'

It was such an extraordinary reply that Callum almost laughed. 'How is that possible?'

'His supernatural imagination speaks to him in numbers and codes and in patterns even I don't understand and I've known a lot of powerful beings in my day.' Orianna reached out and touched Zach's hair, stroking it back from his damp, spangled forehead. 'It is how he animates.'

Callum rubbed his aching temples. 'You still haven't said where we're going.'

'Rome of course.'

Something sparked through Callum. He thought perhaps it was relief, but it was hard to tell. Leaning forward, Orianna put her hands on his knees again, and squeezed.

'Someone will meet us when we land,' she said. 'You'll take them to where you've hidden the map of the Tree of Life so we can destroy its roots.'

Callum flinched from the pressure. 'What about you and Zach?'

'We are expected elsewhere. More whisky?'

*

Sparring with Zach and the Orion plane had given Luca an unexpected thrill. He liked to improvize. It was one of the abilities where he felt his humanity and his Nephilim nature intersected with grace.

He landed silently, cloaked in dusk in his courtyard in Trastevere. He had a concert to prepare for. He headed inside, thoughtfully rubbing the almost imperceptible bump under the skin on his forearm where Zach had implanted the tracking device. Not for the first time in recent days, he was impressed at the young man's ingenuity and courage.

ROME

73.

LITTLE RED CORVETTE

Inside a private hangar at Rome's da Vinci airport, Callum spotted two men: the younger one dressed in torn jeans hanging loose on his hips and a vintage Dylan T-shirt, and the older one in leather trousers and thigh-high boots, looking like he'd stepped out of a Rembrandt painting. Callum eyed the Rembrandt guy with some misgivings, noting the dagger tucked under the waistband of his trousers.

The two men started towards the plane, but the younger one stopped as Zach emerged from the cabin. The air bristled with something indefinable before they walked into each other's arms.

'I wouldn't mind being part of this,' remarked the Rembrandt guy.

'In your dreams, Michele,' came the reply from the dude in the Dylan T-shirt.

'Callum, meet Matt Calder and Michele Merisi da Caravaggio the artist,' said Orianna. 'Close your mouth,' she added in an undertone. 'The flies in Rome are a menace.'

Callum recovered himself. 'Caravaggio?' he said, a little weakly. 'As in, you know, Caravaggio?'

The artist bowed. 'You're adorable,' he said. 'A little stupid, but adorable.'

Orianna reached for Matt, kissing him on both cheeks. 'You're very like your father, you know.' Callum saw Matt wince. 'Before you ask, your sister and our Conjuror are still in America. I'm hoping they'll stay there until this is all over. You know what to do, Matt?'

Matt nodded. 'Vaughn filled us in on everything.' Orianna seemed satisfied.

'Come on, Zach,' she said, gesturing. 'We need to go. We're expected at the Vatican.'

Callum rubbed his eyes when a Range Rover and a sleek red coupe materialized from nowhere. Matt tucked a sketchpad back into his jeans and opened the passenger door of the SUV, motioning for Callum to get in.

'Where are we going?' Callum managed to ask.

'To wherever you hid the map.'

Zach and Orianna swung away from the hangar towards the Vatican in their low-slung red car as Callum directed Matt to the fastest route to the Spanish Steps and the church where he'd hidden the illustration. Caravaggio was in the back. They drove the SUV as close to the church as possible before the three of them jumped out. The church door was locked, but with a quick animation they were inside.

'Have you ever considered burglary as a career?' asked

Callum as they crept down the centre aisle towards the pipe organ.

He ducked under the construction tape and the velvet ropes to retrieve the satchel and its precious contents. No matter what else it represented, it had been Pietra's death warrant.

'May I see it?' asked Caravaggio, wiping his hands on his jacket.

Feeling shy in front of the great artist, Callum opened the portfolio. Caravaggio leaned closer, staring at the head of a grotesque ram growing out of the bulbous trunk of a tree from which multiple branches reached out to pictures of ancient temples.

'That is where the Watchers will rise,' said Caravaggio, reverently pointing to the ram's head.

'Pietra and I always thought it was metaphorical,' Callum said, staring at the image.

'No,' said Caravaggio in a hushed tone. 'It is quite literal. This all lies beneath Rome. This is the Eternal City. Exactly as it is shown.'

Matt was staring at Caravaggio and frowning.

Callum sensed something shifting in the air.

It all happened so fast, it was almost as if nothing had happened at all. Caravaggio replaced the map inside Callum's messenger bag and flipped the bag over his own shoulder. Then, with all the grace of a dancer, he pivoted – and plunged his dagger into Matt's side.

Eyes wide, Matt crumbled to the stone floor.

'*Mi dispiace*,' said Caravaggio. 'But I must go now.'

Matt groaned, clutching his side. He struggled on to his elbows. 'You bastard!' he choked out as the artist ran for the doors. 'I hope Luca tears you apart when he catches you.'

The artist turned back briefly. 'Ah, but you see my friend, that's not going to happen. In return for bringing this map to Cecilia, I will get my life back. The map and, of course, this.'

He produced a rolled-up canvas from his boot and waved it with a faint air of apology. Callum didn't know what the canvas represented, but Matt clearly did.

'The Devil's Interval!' he gasped. 'The painting... you stole it when we were in Kentigern. I have been... so stupid...'

'Yes,' Caravaggio agreed. 'Now there will be no more running for me. No more being hunted. You can see the appeal.' He pulled open the heavy wooden doors. '*Ciao.*'

The dark church echoed with the booming sound of the door as it shut, followed by the artist's disappearing footsteps.

'Why didn't I see it?' Matt's eyes were wild and glazed with pain. 'Too stupid... Too late...'

Callum roused himself. The wound in Matt's side was bleeding. 'Stop moving, man,' he said sharply, pressing his hand against Matt's hip to staunch the flow. 'I need to get help.'

'No time,' groaned Matt. 'Get me something to draw with. We need to find that bloody tree and stop the Inquisitor. But we've lost the map...'

Callum knew the map like the back of his hand. He'd drawn it, inch by inch, labouring late into the night. He could recall every detail, every twisting branch.

'But we've still got a copy.' He tapped his head. 'In here.'

74.

BODY LANGUAGE

Inside a luxurious salon in a wing of the Vatican's private quarters, Cecilia zipped Sol's skin-tight black leather jumpsuit up under her chin, then tugged it down again a couple of inches. Beads of perspiration glistened on Sol's skin. Cecilia pressed a tip of her finger to one of the droplets, bringing the moisture to her own lips, tasting it.

'Nervous?' she said.

Sol smiled. She was dressed as if for battle, her thigh high boots as highly polished as the ceremonial sword at her side, the Camarilla insignia boldly displayed on her back. 'Not a bit. Everyone is here.' She stepped aside to let Cecilia admire herself in the gilded mirror. 'The invitation was impossible to resist. The atmosphere outside is almost rapturous.'

'Wonderful.' Cecilia brushed a loose strand of hair from Sol's forehead and ushered her out of the door. 'You have been an indispensable general in our struggles.

This time we will succeed, and you will be rewarded handsomely. Go now. I'll be there soon.'

When Cecilia turned around, Luca was leaning against the massive marble fireplace.

'I thought I felt a chill in the air,' Cecilia remarked. Her eyes narrowed. 'Do you have it?'

Stepping forward, Luca handed her a rectangular box. She unclasped the lock. Inside the box sat the lyre, its strings shimmering beneath a layer of Bosch's paint dust.

'Good,' she murmured, stroking the lyre. 'Very good.'

She lifted her head. The windows were open wide to the night, and Luca was gone.

Dressed in a black satin *stola* with a diamond clasp on each shoulder and a jewelled crown of laurels expertly set in her up-do, Cecilia looked every inch the Italian couture model. Tilting her head at the long mirror as if seeing herself for the first time, a smile tugged at her plump red lips, her hands running over the curve of her breasts, her slender hips, her toned stomach.

Not for one moment in the past few days had the Inquisitor regretted the decision to inhabit this body.

75.

UNDER PRESSURE

The Basilica looked like a wedding cake, its walls and dome gleaming white with bunting and ribbons of red and gold adorning the façade. Rémy stood outside the metal barricades separating those with the hottest tickets in Rome and those only hoping for a standing view of the concert and perhaps even a glimpse of someone famous. Three massive screens had been set up around the perimeter of the square to broadcast the concert. The Vatican had announced that morning that even the Pope would be attending, and a raised, white-draped section with gold chairs had been installed near the wings of the stage.

The stage itself looked like a long gold tongue, extending into St Peter's Square from the steps to the Basilica. The square was lined with rows of chairs for the invitation-only crowd. There was still an hour before the concert was set to begin, and it looked as if most of Rome's elite had already taken their seats while the rest of the city spilled away into the streets beyond.

Rémy had the static cranked so high on his earbuds that a group of elderly men and women standing next to him glared at the spill-over. He growled at them, and they edged away.

His fury at himself for losing Em had almost killed him back in Louisiana. When he'd crumpled to the marshy ground of the bayou beside the empty, gently rocking boat she had animated for them both, he'd been unsurprised to see the ram's horns he'd given her, lying cracked open on the ground. All that remained was an invitation, pinned like a bad joke to the shattered pitch pipes that had lain within.

GRAND GALA CONCERT

'Black Orpheus'

St Peter's Square, Rome

Come and get her

Raging, Rémy had conjured tickets for flights to New Orleans and on to Rome. Over the Atlantic, he had tried to sleep, but his dreams were angry and disjointed, full of images of monstrous trees and devilish goats chasing him through the bayou while the dead sang to him. He had lost Em. He had lost the pipes: the key to his destiny.

He'd thought about sending a message to Vaughn

and the others, but knew they'd stop him. Alessandro's words echoed in his mind. *The last place you should be is Rome, Rémy. Trust me.* It was risky. But what choice did he have? He couldn't bear the scar of another loved one's death on his heart.

The entirety of St Peter's Square was lit with enormous floodlights that washed the scene in sepia tones. The area was cordoned off with white sawhorses and wire fencing and running outside the perimeter of the security fence was a ring of soldiers. Rémy looked more closely at their uniforms. Every other soldier bore the lyre-insignia of the Camarilla on their flak jackets. They all had earpieces and mics. Rémy was sure they were on the look-out for him.

He backed away from the crowd, straight into someone standing directly behind him. Alessandro pulled Rémy out of the main flood of pedestrian traffic towards the river.

'How did you know I was here?' said Rémy in shock.

Alessandro tapped the golden tablet, the talisman that hung around his neck. 'You were not difficult to find,' he said. The other half of the talisman that Alessandro had given to the mother on the slave ship and that Rémy's mother had centuries later given to him hummed gently against his skin, calling to Alessandro's half.

'I told you to stay away,' said Alessandro, his anger tightening his grip on Remy's arm. 'You could have sent us what you discovered through the… the cyber world. If the Camarilla catch you, they will use you to destroy us all. Vaughn's already got his agents prepared and in place.'

Rémy put his hand on the warm metal. 'Em,' he said softly. 'I think the Camarilla have her.'

'What?'

'Someone took her from the bayou when we were there.' Rémy pulled the invitation from his pocket. 'They left this for me.'

Alessandro stared at the mocking words. The sky above St Peter's was suddenly a maelstrom of lightning, snapping and curling spider webs of silver light through the sky. If Rémy hadn't known better, he'd have sworn it was part of the pre-concert light show. He slipped his mother's journal from under the band of his jeans. 'Take care of this for me. I need to do this alone.'

Alessandro took the book and slid it into the leather pouch across his chest.

'Not this time,' he replied, and his voice was hard. 'This time we do it together.'

76.

CHEAP TRICK

Zach stood anxiously behind the private box and stared out at the people who filled the first three circles around the stage that had been constructed around the Egyptian obelisk in the middle of the square. The air was thick with incense and the unmistakable odour of weed and cigarettes drifting in from the far edges of the square. But it was the stink of arrogance, lust and hunger for power exuding from the seated Camarilla that forced Zach to breathe through his nose.

Zach typed into his tablet.

It's starting. Do you have the map?

The entire square was plunged into darkness. The screens shut down, the spotlights on the stage clicked off. The clouds overhead seemed to thicken and anchor themselves above the stage. The crowd whistled, cheered and stomped their feet in anticipation.

A spotlight clicked on and Cecilia stood centre stage. Cheap trick, thought Zach.

'My dear friends and honoured guests. I am Cecilia Ciardi, and I welcome you to this evening's performance, a concert presentation of *Black Orpheus* in honour of the Museum of Antiquities.' She nodded towards the Pope's private box, where His Holiness, two cardinals, the Italian President, two cabinet members and Fiera Orsini sat. 'You are about to experience a night that will change your lives forever.'

She raised her hands to the heavens. Everything went dark again. A chill wind blew across the square. The ground shook. The hanging clouds parted. And the performance began.

77.

PUPPET SHOW

uca swooped out of the light and over the square, brushing the tips of his wings over the heads of the audience. There was a sharp stink of singed hair. The crowd gasped, and the front rows of Camarilla members fell to their knees. Enjoying himself, Luca soared upwards and, in a flash of fiery light, settled on the dome of St Peter's where he languorously spread his wings and took a bow.

The square exploded with applause. Luca soaked in the accolades, then flew down to the stage where he folded his wings behind his back and raised a finger to his lips.

A hush fell over the crowd.

'You,' he said.

He pointed to a man and woman sitting in the ring of seats behind the Camarilla. With a flick of his wrist, he scooped them into the air and made them dance like marionettes. Their limbs jerked and flopped to the delight of the crowd, until Luca grew bored and set them back on their seats. He did the same with a couple on the other side of the stage, and again, and again, repeating the trick until everyone in the square – bar the Camarilla – was flopping against each other and twitching like herring in a fishing net.

Oh yes. This was exciting. He had shifted his balance. Made his decision.

78.

THE MAIN ATTRACTION

'I have to get closer,' said Rémy, his earbuds blocking out most of the sounds coming from the square.

Alessandro began to protest, but Rémy ignored him. He showed his invitation to a guard and was ushered inside and down one of the aisles. As he moved, a dazzling spotlight hit him full in the face. He put up an arm to protect his eyes even as the circles of Camarilla threw themselves to the ground with a collective gasp.

'Are you still there?' Rémy asked in a low voice as he headed towards the stage.

'Every step of the way,' came Alessandro's reply behind him. 'You know that you will now be the lead in this performance?'

'Yes.'

Luca was waiting on the stage, his arms crossed, his wings folded behind his back. Cecilia was nowhere to be seen.

'Are you sure you know what you're doing?' Alessandro asked.

Rémy shielded his eyes from the light. 'I've seen what I have to do,' he said. 'Find Em and get her away from here, Alessandro. Promise me.'

'You have my word.'

Alessandro melted back into the crowd.

When he reached the stage, Rémy climbed up next to Luca, his heart hammering in his chest. The chant among the Camarilla began, low but distinct.

'*Ecce unus est. Ecce unus est*... Behold the one!'

A great roar echoed around the square.

From the entrance to the Basilica came a rumbling like a monster truck.

79.

HOWL

It wasn't a monster truck. Just a monster.

A slavering she-wolf bounded out of the darkness and into the square, trampling over the incapacitated crowd. Her breath glistened like frost in the warm air, and her breathing was deafening to Rémy who cranked up the sound on his earbuds. Riding on the she-wolf's back was Cecilia, standing upright, holding the wolf's reins as if she were driving a chariot.

The Camarilla were rapturous.

The mark on Rémy's neck was on fire.

80.

RIDE LIKE THE WIND

Across town, Callum had managed to get Matt to his feet and outside. Between the two of them, they'd staunched the bleeding from the wound. Matt had animated a roll of surgical bandages and a tube of sterile glue, and Callum had played nurse.

'Does it hurt?'

'What do you think?'

The animated Range Rover was still outside. Callum helped Matt into the passenger seat and fastened his seatbelt.

'You know this city, right?' Matt gasped. 'Get as close to St Peter's Square as you can.'

Out of the Range Rover window, tornadoes of litter and junk were swirling up into the air. Whatever was happening in St Peter's Square was generating a gale-force wind, sending pedestrians inside for shelter and scooters rocketing off the roads. The wound in Matt's side throbbed as Callum swerved through the flying debris, but Caravaggio's betrayal hurt way worse. The Devil's Interval and the map, both taken from under Matt's nose. His fury blinded him. He kept his shades tight on his face.

81.

ONE NOTE SONG

The she-wolf reached the stage and let Cecilia dismount beside Rémy. She cocked her head at him in a gesture that was both seductive and malevolent.

The First Watcher felt invincible. Her body was strong and athletic and she could feel the power pulsing in her veins. She looked out at her acolytes. What fools they were. Reaching her hands in the air, she quieted their roars.

Sol had appeared, holding a wooden box with the Conjuror's mark on its scarred surface. Inside, a golden lyre lay nestled in silk, its strings yellow with age. It hummed where it lay.

'Play,' Cecilia ordered, lifting the lyre from the box and presenting it to Rémy.

*

The lyre was lighter than Rémy expected. His head rang with its power.

'I will not play anything until I know Em Calder is OK,' he said, as steadily as he could, feeling the pull of the darkness from the instrument.

Cecilia's head swelled as if it had been filled with air, then returned to normal size.

'*Play!*' she shrieked.

Rémy plucked a string reluctantly. The sound was like a gunshot blast, echoing around the square. It was worse inside his own head. It began like the keening of a trapped animal, then became a chorus of wailing and weeping. Not of animals. Of men and women and children. All of human suffering, in one long note.

The ground at his feet opened up. Bluebottle flies swarmed out of the hole. The stage creaked and rocked beneath his feet, fissures stretched out like fingers across the square. The surrounding buildings trembled.

With a superhuman effort, Rémy lowered the lyre. 'No more until I see Em.'

Cecilia snarled. Her eyes matched the feral viciousness of the she-wolf.

'Go then. See her,' she spat.

She raised her arms. An earthquake rocked the square, opening an abyss as wide as the stage itself. The branches of a great white tree emerged from the earth, reaching out into the square like monstrous fingers.

Rémy fell.

82.

EIDETIC

Callum abandoned the Range Rover in front of a loading dock close to the square. He jumped out and ran to the passenger side to Matt, who waved off his help. They jogged towards St Peter's together.

At the high wall surrounding the Vatican, they stopped. The entire area was blocked off, a flotilla of utility vehicles parked like a mechanical moat around the square. The whirlwind was powerful, blasting around them like a raging beast.

'It looks like there's a lid on top of the square,' yelled Matt over the wind, holding his side and craning his neck. 'You can't even see the Basilica dome.'

Another earthquake rocked the area, sending one of the rubbish trucks nose down into the ground and cracking open chunks of pavement.

Matt!

Matt froze where he stood.

'What?' said Callum, alert.

'My sister,' Matt said after a moment. 'She's *inside* that maelstrom. I can feel her in my head.'

'Is this a twin thing? Orianna said you were twins.'

Hardly able to hear Callum through the roar of air, Matt slid down the wall to the pavement, his side exploding in pain. 'Yes. Kind of. We need to get in there.'

Callum crouched in front of Matt. 'I can help.'

'Unless you can climb tall buildings in a single bound, I doubt it.'

'Does an eidetic brain count?'

'Eid… what?'

'I remember things. Photographic memory, you could call it. It's why I'm a good forger.' He said this with some pride. 'You know I said I had the map in my mind? I have literally *all* of it in my mind. Every last detail.'

'Keep talking,' Matt said, interested.

Callum grinned. 'If you give me some charcoal and your sketchpad, I'll draw it.'

Matt held up his hand and let Callum pull him off the ground. He almost lost the sketchpad and charcoal to the ferocious wind blowing all around them, but Callum seized them and drew a rough outline of the map. He turned the page towards Matt. The paper flapped and curled in his hands.

'This bulbous part of the tree: I think it's the portal,' he said. 'And these two branches lead to the centre, here.'

'There's nothing there,' said Matt, gazing at a part of the map that looked like an empty field.

'Back in the day, there was nothing but fields and swamps on this side of Rome. Vatican City eventually built on them. And if I'm reading this correctly, this symbol...' Callum tapped a small mark on the page, '... is Castel Sant'Angelo. The Sistine Chapel is on the north side of St Peter's, so I think the portal is underneath whatever is on the *south* side.'

Still gingerly clutching his side, Matt used his encrypted phone to look up a map of St Peter's. 'That's the Tomb of the Martyrs,' he said. 'Give me back the sketchpad. Now!'

83.

REWIND

Rémy had been here before.

The tomb had been recently rebuilt, the walls no longer the shambles of masonry it had been the last time he'd seen it. The painting *The Flaying of Marsyas* was still hanging on the wall, beside the fluttering tapestry.

In the centre of the tomb was the bulbous trunk as white as alabaster and as bare as a skinned animal with the ram's head of Pan, the God of Nature, growing out of it. The tree's roots were like worms writhing underground. When the thick liquid overflowing from three brass cauldrons met the roots, Pan's head swelled as flesh developed around his fossilized skull.

Rémy looked up and the keening he'd heard from the lyre became his own. Caught in the choking branches like a broken kite was Em, and next to her, bleeding from a wound to his head, was Alessandro.

They were both dead. He was sure of it in his heart and his head.

The tapestry fluttered away from the frieze as two people entered the space. What the hell was Caravaggio doing here? Had the Inquisitor captured Matt, too?

Caravaggio was clasping his hands in supplication as he entered the tomb. He wasn't a prisoner in this performance; he was a willing participant. Jesus, how badly had they all fucked up?

Caravaggio at least had the grace not to look Rémy in the eye. The blonde woman behind him was familiar somehow.

Cecilia Ciardi followed, holding the lyre. Except... it wasn't Cecilia. At least, not the Cecilia Rémy had seen on the stage, holding out her hands to the ecstatic crowd, her black *stola* blowing in the wind. This Cecilia was shedding her skin like a snake. Her head was alive, her scalp covered in hundreds of tiny harpies, their needle-like claws curling out and scratching at the air, their wings fluttering like black hummingbird wings around her face. Rémy felt something cold and metallic clamp around his wrists. He looked down at the manacles, then up again in disbelief.

'You,' he croaked. 'You're the Inquisitor. The First Watcher.'

'I've had many names and many bodies. The old man's was far too weak. This now...' The First Watcher stroked the skin as it peeled away. 'This has suited me well.'

The lyre was thrust into Rémy's manacled hands.

With a flick of long claws, the First Watcher summoned Caravaggio.

'Give him the chord.'

Caravaggio unrolled the canvas he held in his hand. The beautiful colours of his painting *Rest on the Flight into Egypt* glowed in the dim light. He reached in, removed the sheet of music in front of the violin-playing angel and set it in front of Rémy with an ironic half-bow.

'Traitor,' hissed Rémy. He shot out his hand and slashed a manacle across the artist's cheek. Caravaggio leapt back with a howl.

'Play,' hissed the Inquisitor. 'Play and you may still save your other friends.'

The familiar blonde woman reappeared with two young men in leg-irons, their hands cuffed in front of them. Rémy didn't recognize the first guy, who looked pale and frightened. But he sucked the air between his teeth at the sight of the second. Zach – Em's ex, the guy in the camel coat from Chicago – brought up the rear, a tablet tucked under his arm.

84.

THE TREE OF LIFE

The blood oozing from Matt's side was making him dizzy. He couldn't understand how he came to be here. One moment he and Callum had been making their way through the tunnel beneath the Tomb of the Martyrs, and the next... A flash, a sense of the world turning upside-down... and then the unmistakeable chill of iron manacles on his wrists and ankles. He'd lost his sunglasses. Thank God it was dim in here. Unsteadily, he raised his head and stared at the vast white tree growing in the centre of the room. Its topmost branches had breached the ground far above his head, and were stretching into a dark and thunderous sky. What in God's name was hanging up there? It looked like...

The frenzied flash from his kaleidoscopic eyes was so bright with horror that Caravaggio, Callum and Zach raised their hands to protect their own vision. The Inquisitor roared, and waved a claw that hurled Matt and Callum back against the stone wall. Blessed darkness descended.

85.

WAITING

Zach struggled to control himself at the sight of Em hanging sightlessly in the hideous breathing tree. He felt a hand on his back. It wasn't yet time. If he acted too soon, everything they had planned would be for nothing. He closed his eyes.

He let his mother's touch calm him.

86.

BEHOLD, THEY RISE

'Play!' The Inquisitor sloughed off more of Cecilia's body, revealing scales as black as pitch, the head of a reptile and compound insect eyes.

Swallowing his revulsion, Rémy stared at the piece of music before him. It didn't matter. Nothing did now. Em was dead. Alessandro too. Matt lay unconscious on the ground. Vaughn had no idea where they were. They were all lost.

He plucked the chord.

The tree stretched seductively like a panther on the prowl, its limbs extending up to the light. The viscous liquid continued to spill over the roots and carpeted the stones of the vault. Rémy's eyes were wet with tears, but through them he watched two similar reptilian creatures crawl from the thickening fog spewing from beneath the roots of the tree.

87.

DOWN IN FLAMES

Zach slipped his tablet from under his arm and began silently to tap the screen. From the corner of his eye he saw his mother flick her left wrist in a curious motion. There was a shriek from the creeping Watchers, and a burst of white flame. The trunk of the tree hissed and spat as it caught alight.

Zach stopped tapping. Since when could his mother shoot fire? She was a Guardian, not a magician.

88.

WE THREE

Cecilia was nothing more than clots of flesh on the ground. The Inquisitor swung round to face the blonde flame-thrower.

'Sol!' he roared. 'What is the meaning of this disobedience?'

The blonde woman smiled. 'Sol has served her purpose, Father. Don't you recognize me? It's been an age, I know...'

Another blast of flame hit the ground, sparking the silver liquid into giant shards of flying ice.

'Sebina?' The Inquisitor's croaking voice was incredulous. 'You defied me?'

'I choose life...' She looked at Zach. 'And love.'

Hissing, the Inquisitor raised its scaly arms before the hurtling fireballs and stabbing blades of ice. Harpies emerged from its claws, enveloping everyone in the room, pecking at their eyes like buzzards.

Sol – Sebina – *Orianna*. She flicked her wrists again.

This time, silver mist emerged. The harpies froze and fell to the ground.

The tree was no longer growing, flames lapping at its roots, the other Watchers shrivelling to ashes.

89.

ART AND LIFE

Rémy was glad of the fire. It brought him back to his senses. The flames coiled around the rising tree, searing its smooth white bark, cauterizing it. They licked at the edges of the tapestry that covered the wall. The ancient fabric curled and burned away like paper, revealing the stone frieze beneath. And there he was again, being crowned King of the Underworld. Ambuya's mirror had shown Rémy this scene as it had first unfolded. He would not let it become reality, even if he died resisting.

The carved goddess with the pipes stretched her marble limbs. She caught his eye – and winked.

Minerva. The pipes.

Rémy dropped the lyre and crawled to the frieze through the billowing smoke. He reached up, knowing that the stone would part before his manacled hands. He had lost the pipes the day that he had won the contest against Apollo inside *The Flaying of Marsyas*. He had asked to keep them as his prize, but hadn't thought about them again until this moment.

It was as if they had been waiting for him in the tomb for all this time.

90.

ALTERED STATES

Zach stood, paralysed, one hand hovering over his screen. Sebina was the name from the curious message he had passed to Luca in the café from Orion. He could hear Luca in his head, even now. The hope in the Nephilim's voice. *Sebina is alive?*

His mother gestured at him with a free hand. *Don't freeze now! Do it!*

He blindly keyed in one last line of code.

The ground suddenly shook as Luca dropped from the square above, his wings blocking the light. Caravaggio shrieked and cowered into a ball.

'You are mine, artist,' Luca hissed. 'You are responsible for Sebina's death. You and you alone. I will make you wish you had never been born.'

Sebina. That name again. Zach's brain was stuck on the revelation that Sebina, Sol, Orianna, were one and the same.

His mother.

Off to the side of the tomb, he saw Caravaggio sliding to his feet. Rousing himself, Zach body-slammed the artist against the wall. Lifting his hands to the artist's terrified face, he flickered his fingers.

Going somewhere?

He shoved the artist to the ground, placing a foot on his neck. A hologram cage hovered above his tablet, expanded like a balloon and dropped over his captive with a metallic clang.

With an emphatic jab on the screen, the hologram began to shrink. Caravaggio screeched in shock as the image closed around him. He dissolved into dusty pixels and disappeared.

91.

SOUL DEEP

The Inquisitor swung to face Rémy, stone cold eyes staring.

'Where did you get those pipes? I took them form the girl. I *destroyed* them!'

Feeling the coolness of the ivory against his palm, Rémy put the pipes to his lips and played.

The roots of the tree pulled themselves from the ground, revealing a deep green abyss below. With a roar, the Inquisitor sent more harpies at Rémy's head.

Luca unfurled his silver-black wings in the small space, and swooped at the Inquisitor, wrapping him in his blazing light and concealing him from view. The harpies vanished in a puff of smoke.

Luca turned to the others. 'It's complicated,' he said.

He tipped sideways. He and the Inquisitor plunged into the abyss.

'No!'

Rémy turned at the strangled yell. Zach had thrown

himself to the edge of the abyss, reaching with one desperate hand to the blonde woman as she was sucked down into the underworld with Luca and the Inquisitor in a surge of air. Too late.

Rémy closed his eyes and let the pipes' notes rise to a crescendo.

Flames ate what was left of the trunk.

The abyss crept shut like a wound healing itself, leaving only shrivelling, charred roots like skeletal fingers gripping the ground.

92.

A SONG FOR THE DEAD

Rémy used Minerva's pipes to conjure open his manacles, then freed Callum and Matt from their leg irons as they slowly regained consciousness. Zach sat beside the space where the abyss had been, holding his head in his hands. Alessandro's body had fallen awkwardly.

Rémy crawled over to Em and cradled her in his arms. Her skin was cold, her lips and nails blue. He swept the pink streaked hair from her face, took her hand and held it to his cheek, then against his heart.

Music gives life to the dead.

Not a prophecy. Not a curse.

A legacy.

Rémy opened his mouth and sang the song he'd heard the little girl singing on the doomed slave ship. Nuru's song. It carried in its chords the cries of her ancestors and the hopes of her children, the melody flowing from his Conjuror's soul.

A golden mist of music curled around the fallen tree branches. It widened and spread, enveloping the vault and lifting all of them into the light and space of St Peter's Square. Rémy didn't stop singing until his throat was raw.

The golden veil of mist lifted. Em was sitting up against the obelisk in the centre of the square. And she was breathing.

93.

FAMILY AFFAIR

The square was utterly quiet, still full of a silent crowd, and chairs, and a long golden stage that had been broken in two. As the mist spread, they began to stir as if roused from some form of hypnosis. Waves of people stumbled delirious and dizzy towards the exits, where not one Camarilla soldier remained at their post.

Callum and Matt had landed beside the Basilica steps. Callum walked awkwardly, holding his arm, but Matt ran towards the obelisk, the bloody bandage around his waist trailing behind him.

'Thank God,' he said, hugging Em. 'I thought for sure you were dead. It felt in my head like you were.'

Em studied the fingernails of her free hand. They were an odd shade of blue. 'I'm pretty sure I have a concussion, but that's all.' She looked up at Rémy, who held her other hand. 'Right?'

Rémy's heart ached for Alessandro even as he remembered his words. *Some secrets are ours to keep.*

'Right,' he said. 'I'm sure that's all.'

'We need to get you all away from here.'

Rémy looked up to see a slender, white-haired woman raise her cane in the air. A black SUV crashed through the rubble surrounding the square and pulled up next to the obelisk. He stood slowly, helping Em to her feet. Matt and Callum walked together, supporting one another as they climbed into the car.

Still sitting on the far side of the square, Zach hadn't moved. Rémy recalled the way the blonde woman had vanished into the abyss, and how Zach had screamed for her. He glanced at the white-haired woman, who was watching Zach with compassionate eyes.

Without warning, an aftershock cracked across the square. Two colonnades crashed to the ground and a cloud of choking debris swirled into the air. With his wings open behind him, Luca walked out of the curtain of grey with the blonde woman at his side. They appeared to be holding hands. Rémy remembered where he'd seen her now: when he had been trapped in the ancient tomb. She was Zach's mother.

Zach looked up. His mother broke into a smile, then a run. As she embraced Zach, Luca swept them both off the ground and into the air, his wings scorching the night sky.

It seemed that Zach didn't need a ride.

94.

IN MY TIME OF DYING

In the darkness above Constantine's Arch, a slit of white light opened up in the sky and Luca descended, carefully carrying his precious human cargo. He set Sebina and the young man gently down on the masonry, and stroked Zach's hair.

Zach took one look at the drop, and was sick over the side of the monument. Sebina put her arms around Zach's shoulders and turned his face towards hers. He resisted at first, but then relented. They held each other as Luca watched.

'It seems you've been keeping secrets from me,' Luca said at last.

Sebina smiled. 'Zach is my son, Luca,' she said. 'The apple never falls far from the tree. He is a master at subterfuge, animating firewalls and inspiriting. He had Cecilia wrapped around his fingers from the beginning.'

The darkness swirled around them like a tornado. Luca moved closer to Sebina, afraid that she would vanish before his eyes. He touched her face, stroked the soft skin of her neck, wrapped a strand of her hair around his fingers. Then he laughed, a sound that cracked the few windows nearby that the recent earthquakes hadn't broken.

'My love,' he said in wonder. 'We have endured.'

He pulled her into his arms and lifted her back into the air, feeling her body warm against his. The clouds rumbled and fingers of horizontal lightning shot across the sky.

'I've been sick without you,' Luca murmured, pressing his lips to her hair as they sank back down on to the top of the arch beside Zach. 'Why did you hide for so long? How was it that you were helping Orion?'

'We shared a similar ambition. To destroy the Inquisitor.'

Luca could understand that.

'The Duke of Albion and the Order of Era Mina saved my life,' Sebina went on. 'They created an animation to be executed in my place. We knew the Inquisitor would not die easily. And so I made a deal: to be bound in a painting until our common purpose came to pass. Then the Order would strike. And so would I. I was released when the Conjuror, Rémy, was born. I knew the final battle was coming.'

Luca frowned. 'Orion knew twenty years ago that this might happen?'

'They had contacts in America. Word spread that Rémy Dupree Rush would be a Conjuror unlike any other. A Conjuror to raise the Second Kingdom, or if we were lucky destroy it. There was no way of telling which.'

Zach tapped his mum's shoulder. 'Who,' he signed, and then corrected it to: '*What* are you?'

'Still your mum,' she signed back with a kiss. 'Just a bit older than I look.' She turned back to Luca. 'I spent four hundred years bound in a portrait in the Abbey at Auchinmurn's vaults,' she said quietly. 'Four hundred years of thinking about the last thing someone said to me.'

'Which was?'

Her eyes were bleak. 'You are forgiven.'

95.

MIDNIGHT CONFESSIONS

Sebina hadn't thought of Brother Ignatius Gallo in a long time. She hoped he'd lived a long life. She knew he had taken her secret to his grave, because no one in her former life, not even Luca, had ever guessed that she was still alive.

She had been imprisoned in the catacombs of the Basilica di Santa Maria shortly after she and Luca had lost Caravaggio and the Devil's Interval, and chained to a wall that ran wet with piss from a courtyard above. Her head was locked beneath a hammered gold scold's bridle, and any movement tore the skin from her scalp and punctured her cheeks, the taste of her own blood her only nourishment. Until the old monk appeared.

Brother Gallo had poured water gently into the bridle so that it pooled under her chin, allowing her tongue to lap it up a little at a time. He came again, and again. He brought her sustenance, and something she didn't know she needed or wanted: forgiveness.

'To lighten another's suffering is my path to God,' he'd told her.

On his fourth visit, Sebina felt a human emotion that shocked her. Shame. It burrowed into her like a leech. She'd eased no one's suffering. She'd only caused it.

A lot of it.

On his fifth visit, Brother Gallo had smuggled a book of poetry inside the cell under his cassock. He had read to her, his head pressed close to hers as if in prayer. When he finished, she found that salt tears had mingled with the fresh water in her bridle.

She remembered most the ash covering Brother Gallo's cassock when he had helped her into a small boat and, like Moses, sent her down the Tiber, out of Rome, to safety, to be bound in a painting until she'd faded from the memory of everyone who had known her.

Or – it seemed – *almost* everyone.

*

'I did many terrible things in my long life on Earth,' she said now. 'Four hundred years of considering your sins makes a difference to a person. When I came out, I hated myself.

'During my first months in this world, Vaughn and I grew close. He was lonely and sad, and I was broken.' She smiled at Zach. 'And you were the result. If I wasn't sure of my destiny before, it was clear the moment you were born. I could not let you live in a world controlled by the Camarilla.'

'So Vaughn is my biological father?' Zach signed, a little shakily, but somehow not surprised.

'Yes.'

Luca stood. 'We should go.' He swept them both into his arms.

'Where?'

'Home.'

LONDON

96.

TO THE MISSING

The Kitten sisters hadn't hosted this many people for dinner in years.

It was two days since the destruction of the tomb, and the Raphael Terrace dining room was aglow with candlelight and conversation. There was a blazing fire in the hearth despite the warmth outside, and the lit sconces on the walls washed the Victorian room in a fitting aura of gold.

Em's dress was a sleeveless dark blue sheath, its cut showing off her toned shoulders and arms. She couldn't remember the last time she'd worn a dress. She was feeling a strange cocktail of emotions. Contentment that Zach was back in her life even if he wasn't here at the party; excitement that they'd destroyed the Inquisitor; and a spike of desire every time she caught Rémy looking across the room at her.

The sideboard was spread with silver platters of bacon-wrapped figs, stuffed mushrooms, plump shrimp and a vast array of cheeses and meats. In front of the spread, Matt and Callum were chatting, both dressed in variations on the same theme of black shirts and skinny jeans. In the middle of the large room, Anthea was fussing with the table settings on the long elegantly dressed table, the light twinkling brilliantly off the crystal glasses from the candelabra in the centre.

'You look beautiful,' Rémy said, handing Em a glass of champagne.

'You clean up nicely too,' she said, smiling.

The attraction between them sizzled in the air as Matt joined them at the fireplace.

'Get on and kiss already,' he advised.

Em frowned at her brother. 'Mattie? Stay out of my head and my business.'

Matt laughed, his eyes flickering like diamonds in the light. 'It doesn't take a mind-reader to see what you're thinking.'

From across the room, Violet closed the dining-room doors and tapped her champagne glass. 'May I ask you all to take your places?' she called over the hubbub.

'Shouldn't we wait for Vaughn?' said Em.

'He's still in Rome, working on clean-up with Fiera Orsini. And I will not keep chef from serving on time.'

The sisters sat at either end of the table as the meal began. Rémy and Matt sat down one long side, with Em and Callum opposite. An empty place was laid mid-way down the table.

Em leaned close to Callum as they moved through the first course. 'Is your dad joining us?'

'God, I hope not,' said Callum, lifting his wine glass awkwardly with his left hand, not yet used to the cast on his right arm from when he'd hit the wall in the tomb. 'I'm still working up to that reunion.'

Em put her hand on his. 'You'll be fine.'

'I know.' His voice caught in his throat. 'I just wish Pietra had survived. You'd have really liked her.' He looked across the table at the others. 'She'd have liked all of you.'

Rémy lifted his glass. 'To Pietra. Who found what we needed to save the world.'

'To Pietra!' they said, glasses raised in unison.

'And Alessandro,' Rémy added. His heart broke every time he thought of his mentor and protector. 'Who died to save us all.'

'To Alessandro!'

The main course passed without incident, and was as delicious as any meal ever was in the Kitten household. But when they reached dessert, a sudden crash from the other side of the house caught everyone's attention.

'What was that?' said Rémy.

'I'm sure it's nothing,' said Violet, nodding to the waiter to serve the pudding.

Matt and Rémy were on their feet as a chill mist seeped into the room through the panelled walls. The painting of the suffragettes above the fireplace banged

346

against the wall and the shutters on the tall leaded glass windows flew open.

'That is *definitely* something,' said Rémy, staring at the rattling dining-room doors.

97.

CLOOTIE DUMPLING

The doors flew open and Jeannie marched into the room in full Highland dress. Em screamed; Matt leapt to his feet.

'Sorry I'm late,' Jeannie said, unfazed. 'I thought I'd join you, but I forgot how exhausting all this fading can be.' She turned to the looming waiter. 'Whisky please. And make it a double.'

When everyone had recovered from the shock and the clootie dumpling and cream had been served, Jeannie filled in the blanks.

'Two things underscored our plan. The first was Luca Ferrante. We knew that he was more committed to taking his revenge on Caravaggio and the Camarilla than to enslaving the world. We decided to exploit that. We sent Zach to join his mother undercover with the Camarilla. Zach's position also gave us the chance to tag Luca and follow him in case he double-crossed us.'

Jeannie smiled down the table at Rémy. 'But for

everything else we owe a debt to your mum, Rémy. It was her journal that did most of the heavy lifting.' She lifted her glass in Rémy's direction. 'A toast to Annie Dupree Rush. May she rest in peace and may her voice live on.'

'To Annie!'

Sensing Rémy's tightly held emotions, Em rested her head against his shoulder.

'When Cecilia announced her concert,' said Jeannie, 'we knew that would be the Camarilla's moment. We had to use Orianna and Zach and bring things to a head. With their help, we knew in advance about Luca's mission to put an end to the Order of Era Mina.'

'And you emptied the vaults and the Council Chamber before Luca destroyed them,' Em guessed.

'Ach, Em,' said Jeannie comfortably. 'You didn't think we'd destroy the art on purpose? Your grandfather would have strangled us all. Although I must admit, there were one or two members of the Council I would happily have seen vaporized that day.'

'Why?' asked Matt.

Jeannie sighed. 'They refused to accept what was happening until I showed them this.'

She reached into her purse that was tucked under her chair. One by one they passed a photograph around the table.

It was a collage of four clear and convincing images taken at dawn in Rome while the sun was an orange ball rising through the ruins. In the first image, a brooding Luca was crouched naked on top of the Arc of Constantine, his head bowed, his hair draped over his shoulders. In the second, the photographer had caught Luca standing with his black and silver wings unfolding as he began his transformation to his divine form, preparing to take flight. The third image caught Luca's silhouette against the rising sun like Icarus. The final photograph was taken at a distance. It was Luca in human form dressed in a black suit and white shirt escorting a portly older man in an Italian military uniform up the steps of the Museum of Antiquities.

The man was looking back, unaware of a camera snapping photographs from a building across the way. Luigi Silvestri, Sir Giles' second-in-command on the European Council of Guardians was caught at an angle, but there was no doubt it was him.

'Zach took the pictures,' said Jeannie with a smile.

This time Em lifted her glass first. 'To Zach!'

This was not as it turned out the final toast of the night. The celebration continued well into the wee hours of the next morning.

AMERICA

TWO MONTHS LATER

98

TEN MISSISSIPPI

Em carried a tray of mint juleps out on to the wide veranda, a sticky breeze rustling the hem of her cotton dress. Her feet were bare and her skin had erupted in freckles. She set the tray on a wicker table and leaned over Matt's shoulder to take a closer look at the canvas he was working on.

'Mattie, it's stunning.'

'Think so?' He accepted a drink, his cargo shorts hung low at his hips, the wound at his side a red puckered scar. 'It's amazing what I can see when I control the light.'

Matt's shades were doing nothing more than holding his hair from his face. It was as if he was capturing the landscape spread out in front of him in the present and the past. The trees dripped with moss like history was weighing down their limbs, and the brush strokes creating the old wooden hut at the end of the dock looked like children at its windows.

'Do you think Annie knew she had the information about the deed to the Dupree Plantation house and its land tucked into the extra pages of her journal all along?' Em asked.

Matt shrugged. 'I think there's a lot Annie didn't realize, but I'm glad Rémy's found his home.'

Em left him mixing colours and walked around to the other side of the veranda, where a porch swing creaked in the breeze. Eyes closed, Rémy lay stretched out on it, his hands crossed on top of his chest, his guitar standing against the wooden railing.

Em set the ice-cold bottom of the glass on his forehead. His eyes snapped open and he grabbed her hand and pulled her on top of him, spilling his drink.

'I do declare,' she said in an exaggerated southern accent, 'you've ruined mah party dress.'

'Let me make it better.' Rémy kissed her, his lips lingering before he righted himself and she sat next to him. They rocked in silence for a beat, looking out through the palm fronds and the beech trees to the island in the river where Callum could be seen in diving gear on the deck of a professional salvage barge.

'They should be able to refloat the ship in the next few days,' said Rémy. 'Then we'll transport the bones back to Europe and Africa.'

Em pulled her dress over her head, revealing more freckles and a bikini underneath. 'I'm going for a swim out in the bay. Want to join me?'

'You know what?' said Rémy, stretching out across the swing again. 'I think I'd like to wallow in the quiet for just a little longer. For the first time in my life, my head is at peace.'

*

Five thousand miles away, eight-year-old Wesley Brown was staring out the window of a Delta 747 as it began its descent into Rome's Leonardo da Vinci airport. The plane shook violently then rocked to one side, popping open the overheard compartments and dropping the oxygen masks.

'Don't worry, folks,' said the pilot's voice comfortably. 'Just a little turbulence. We'll circle back around and make another approach.'

'That wasn't turbulence,' said Wesley. 'Look.'

His mom looked out the window. She could have sworn she saw an angel somersaulting off the tip of the wing.

Glossary

Animare: A person who can bring their art to life, and who can move in and out of art.

Binding: Binding is a kind of suspended animation. Animare are bound into a work of art as a last resort when they lose control of their powers or endanger the secret of their existence. There are secure vaults all over the world containing bound paintings.

Conjuror: The descendant of an ancient African bloodline with power to alter reality with music and song.

Council of Guardians: A body of powerful Guardians who enforce the Five Rules for Animare. There are five Councils scattered around the world.

1. Animare must not animate in public.
2. They must always be in control of their imaginations.
3. If they endanger the secret of their existence, they may be 'bound' (see above).

4. They are forbidden from having children with Guardians (see below), as this can result in dangerous hybrids with an unpredictable mix of powers.
5. Children cannot be bound.

Guardian: A Guardian has supernatural powers of mind-control. A Guardian's ability to influence a person's thinking is known as 'inspiriting'. Council members do not always agree about how Animare should be guided. When hybrid children are created, for example, some Guardians believe that their talents should be nurtured; while others believe that binding (see above) is the only safe course of action.

The Order of Era Mina: The monks in medieval Auchinmurn belonged to the Order of Era Mina, which had a particular mission: locking away the monsters of the superstitious past by drawing them into a bestiary called *The Book of Beasts*, thereby reinventing the world as a modern place of enlightenment and learning.

Acknowledgements

Before you leave these pages, we'd like you to join us in applauding a few members of Team Barrowman who helped make this book possible. Lucy Courtenay, our brilliant editor, has worked with us on six books and has brought insight and energy to each one. Three big cheers, Lucy!

Exploding high fives to everyone at Head of Zeus, particularly Laura Palmer and Madeleine O'Shea, our agent, Georgina Capel, and the indispensable Kelsey Work.

A rousing standing ovation to our husbands, Kevin Casey and Scott Gill, our parents, Marion and John Barrowman, and our personal cheering section, Clare, Casey, Finn and Adeline, Turner and Hannah.

Finally, if you'd like to learn more about the art and the music in *Inquisitor*, please visit www.barrowmanbooks.com

With love,
Carole and John 2018